MISSING IN ACTION

TASK FORCE 779 BOOK 1

KL DONN

INTRODUCTION

This has been a long time coming you guys.

I wanted to take a quick minute to explain why...

I started writing Missing in Action in April of 2017... 10 years after I lost my baby. There was 10 years of regret... 10 years of pain... 10 years of sorrow piled into the prologue of this story.

Everything I felt when I was 20 years old and losing a child I wasn't ready for has been poured into this story. All of Codie's feelings of self doubt, fear, pain... the damage that course's through her veins...

It's all mine.

The anxiety and helplessness was so overwhelming for so long that when I finally started this journey with Ryder and Codie, I didn't think I would make it to the end.

And now here I am, finalizing Missing in Action on April 16th, 2019, exactly 12 years after hearing the words – you lost the baby – and I'm more than ready to share this journey with you.

I hope you have tissues, because you're going to need them.

Thanks for not giving up on me when I kept putting MiA off.

XOXO
    Krystal

SYNOPSIS

Ryder Morrison is a man of loyalty. To his country, his family, his team.

After joining the Navy, he was secretly recruited to Task Force 779, a specialized unit that infiltrates dangerous situations when no one else can—or will. As the communications expert, it's his job to clear the way for a smooth mission. He knows where the enemy is hidden at all times and when his team can enter a zone safely.

When things go wrong and he's captured, declared dead before a search can truly begin, Ryder knows that when he makes his way home, his life will be different...better. He'll live for himself from now on, instead of following where duty takes him.

Enter his elusive neighbor...
A woman of mystery and fear.

Codie Ray is a woman filled with pain. Afraid of life and locked away.

She counts to soothe the anxiety. She watches her neighbor because he's her only lifeline to the outside world. He's a commitment she doesn't have to worry will break her. Until the unthinkable happens and her solace is intruded upon.

Ryder comes to the rescue and barges his way into her life, pushing past her barriers, causing Codie to rethink her reclusive lifestyle. Slowly being tormented with mind games from an unknown predator, she battles her better judgment and trusts Ryder to do what he does best...hunt down the perpetrator.

Their connection is instantaneous. Two broken people yearning to be loved but afraid to reach for it. Codie fears Ryder will leave when he discovers just how damaged she is. Ryder worries Codie will remain locked away in her mind, unable to break free.

A surprise mission brings both of their fears to life, and when the walls crumble, Ryder is Missing in Action while Codie is just...missing. Will they find each other again or will they disappear, existing only in a memory?

DEDICATION

Codie Louise
My crazy Aussie girl
Codie Ray gets her strength from you
Her resilience is yours
The optimism in a dark time is brought on by your humor,
your love, and your general desire to make the world more
than what it is
Codie, this one's for you

"*P*ush, Codie, you have to push harder!" I want to slap the insensitive doctor upside her fool head as she yells at me.

Don't they get it? I don't want to push. Pushing will make it real.

All the pain and suffering from the past twenty-four hours have left me a shell of skin and bones.

I don't want to push.

"I can't," I cry, and a nurse comes to me with a cool cloth to dab my overheated face. The pain that's continually ripping through me is almost unbearable.

The hurt I'll feel soul deep in the next few minutes will be consuming.

"Please, Codie, just one more, and it will all be over," the doctor pleads again.

I look around the room, and all I see is pity. They know what's about to happen. The insurmountable suffering that'll occur when they hand him to me.

They know there won't be a cry of life.

That first breath of air that should fill his tiny lungs was taken away before he could experience it.

They know this is my last day of feeling anything but agony.

I won't survive it, and yet, I push anyways. They count, *one, two, three.* My tears are mixed with my cries, and I forge on. My mind drifts to a time when I felt his little foot kicking me. When he'd roll over and press on my bladder just as I was falling to sleep. To the morning sickness at three a.m. I'd take it all over again just to watch his chest rise and fall.

It won't happen, and I'm living a nightmare, only digging myself deeper into depression as I think of all the firsts we'll never get to have.

I wasn't ready for a baby. I had been barely seventeen when he came along, but with time, I wanted him more than anything else in my life. I ached to hold and kiss him. Cuddle him when he got cranky.

I wanted him to be my entire world.

Not shatter it.

"Nurse," the doctor calls, handing my son off to her as he's finally free from my body. I can't bear to look, so I turn away, silent tears streaming down my face.

"Codie?" I gaze at the doctor. "One more push to expel the placenta." Her words are hushed.

My body does as she asks, but my mind checks out. I'm selfish, and I hate it. I hate myself for getting into this predicament in the first place. I shouldn't have trusted idiotic Jason Jones when he said he loved me. I was stupid and naïve. His parents tossed a couple hundred bucks at me to abort my baby. I refused; they moved. I don't even know where to. I do know that I'm left to clean up the mess.

My parents kicked me out, and I've been roaming from shelter to shelter up until the last few weeks when a social worker found me begging for food behind some Chinese restaurant. She'd taken me in, fed, and clothed me. Amber became the family I'd never really been given.

Recently, she had to go back home because her dad had a heart attack. I didn't want to bother her when I realized something was wrong with the baby, so I kept quiet and came here alone. I hadn't felt him moving in quite a while, and the baby website I'd found said it wasn't normal and to get to the hospital.

I was rushed to the maternity ward where two nurses and a doctor have been with me ever since. Now, here I am broken, lost, and alone. I wish Hell would open up and take me away.

"Codie," a nurse says quietly, "would you like to hold your son?"

No! Yes, comes out instead. She smiles at me like it's some happy fucking occasion. As my little one is placed in my arms, my entire soul shatters. I'll never get it back. It'll go to the grave with my baby boy. "What will happen to him?" I ask the nurse as she sits next to me.

"Would you like to name him?" she inquires instead of answering me.

My gaze drifts to his tiny body. His tender head with my nose and lips. Perfect chubby cheeks. Dark fuzzy hair only starting to grow on his head. I wish I could have known him. He would have been strong; he'd have made me proud. He was supposed to be the one good thing in my life.

"Lucas," I say, and a sob, so loud it startles the other nurses in the room, rips from deep within me. Pouring all the pain and heartache I feel into the one single sound.

The nurse grabs my hand, squeezing and offering her support as she explains what will happen to my sweet boy. As she lists my options, I notice her own sadness, and I'm left to wonder how many times she's had to recite this very same information to other parents, and briefly, I offer her my support for her own pain.

Ryder

Wiping the sweat from my brow, I silently curse as my team waits for word on whether we move in or not. We've been staking out a Syrian drug lord for nearly six weeks because the asshole keeps setting up sweatshops and forcing underage kids to work for him.

Sometimes they would make cheap clothes or shoes. Other times, like now, they were cooking meth and heroine. Two things kids should never know exist.

I've been tasked with finding out as much intel as I can. As the IT expert on our team, I get the fun job of sitting in hot fucking huts while the rest of my crew hunts these bastards down.

Being part of Task Force 779—yeah, that's it, just a number—is the best and worst part of my life. No one can know I was recruited straight off the ship that I was assigned to after boot camp three years ago. However, I get to bring hope to the helpless. I free hostages, take out drug rings. Track weapons and terrorists from all over the world.

What we do might not be acknowledged by any branch of the service but my team and the President himself, but we don't do it for the glory or fame. We do it because no one else is capable of maneuvering into the situations we are placed in.

Working behind the computer often leaves me feeling unfulfilled. Like I'm not doing enough. Even though without my knowledge and hacking skills, my team wouldn't be able to get into some of the places they do.

"Tac, where's he at?" Out team leader, Nix 'Knot' Bishop, asks me through our comms.

"Southwest corner, basement," I relay back to him. I don't think Nix has called me by my real name since the day we met. Because of my position and expertise on our team, he's switched it to Tac, and it's stuck ever since.

"Close to a window?" Knot asks.

Zooming in on the infrared device attached to the drone I have hovering above the grounds, I check his position and compare it to the floor plans displayed on another screen in front of me.

"Three feet, dead center."

"Phantom, you have the green light," Knot tells Theo Burkhart, our team sniper. He hasn't missed a shot in his ten years in the business. He's called Phantom because no one ever knows he's around until the shots are fired, and they never see him leave.

Silence reigns as Phantom does his thing. A puff of

air and a man seen falling on my screen is the only indication that he's taken the shot.

"One down, Tac."

"Where's the second in command?" Knot asks roughly, sounding slightly out of breath.

"Find yourself a friend, Knot?" Phantom asks as I search for the missing target.

"Big fucking bastard," our team leader complains.

"Gotcha," I murmur as I see the scumbag running for the back shed. "Heads up, Chaos. He's coming your way in 5, 4, 3, 2—" A loud boom shakes the ground as Foster Halsey sets off an explosive device.

"Cocksucker," he grumbles. "I wasn't done with that one."

"How the hell weren't you done? That son of a bitch knocked me on my ass," Weston "Shaker" Green, our team medic, complains. For such a careful and selective man, he always finds himself a little too close to Chaos' homemade devices.

"Stay the hell back when I'm playing then. Pussy." Chaos tends to get pissy when we distract him from building a bigger explosive than is often necessary.

"Did you take that guy out or what?" Knot snaps. He's all for joking around and letting off steam, but only once the mission is finished.

"Yeah, he's flying in the breeze now." Chaos chuckles.

"Rendezvous in ten, and we're out of here," Knot informs us. "Tac, what's the ETA on our helo?"

"Fifteen minutes out." I'm distracted as I'm checking over the device that Chaos left for me to blow up the tiny shack I've been sequestered in and then removing my existence from this dessert hell that I don't hear someone entering behind me.

It isn't until I feel a prick in my neck that I spin around and see three masked men with rifles in their hands pointed at me. As I reach for my sidearm, my arms become sluggish, my head spins, and it feels like I'm floating through a tunnel as they speak to me.

"Tac?" I can hear Knot calling through my comm. "Goddammit, Morrison, answer me!" I recognize the worry and anger in his voice.

Steadying myself, I'm able to get one single thought out, "Get on that helo, sir," before blackness takes me under.

CHAPTER 1
Coodie

Three years later

*Y*ou can do this.
        One more step.
        Keep going.

My body sways forward as my feet stop dead in their tracks. My life wasn't supposed to be like this. I was supposed to be happy, healthy. The world was going to be my oyster!

Until it wasn't.

Now, I'm this little nobody girl that can barely function. I have no friends. No family. Nothing but the UPS man that delivers my packages and the girl that delivers my groceries each week.

I'm nobody.

I'm nothing.

I'm the freak the entire block talks about. The stupid girl that can't leave her house. The girl with no courage. The day I lost Lucas, my whole life spiraled out of control. I couldn't focus long enough to put one foot in front of the other.

When I lost my baby, I thought, for a fleeting moment, that my family would accept me again. I thought they would help me heal.

I was wrong. I'm always wrong. Everyone in my life that I should have ever been able to count on has let me down.

And so, I've moved half way across the country from Rapid City, South Dakota to a busy, unexplored city. In fact, since arriving in Charleston, West Virginia, I haven't done anything outside of my home.

The shrink I speak to on the phone once a week says I'm borderline agoraphobic, and I need to try and push myself to step outside. Open the windows. Feel the sun on my skin. She cautions that the moment I take that first step, I'll be so overcome by such deep and intense emotion that I'll have a panic attack, and that it's okay. That I should embrace it until I can't anymore.

She asked me to open the door today, take three steps back, and count to thirty before giving in to my need to lock myself inside once again. I'm standing within reach of the door handle, just one step closer, and I could open it.

One step.

Only one.

Except... I can't.

I'm paralyzed by fear that when I breach that barrier, that when I feel the breeze and the sun, I'll be consumed by Lucas. His loss. His tiny body in my arms. I'm terrified I won't be able to climb back out of the depression I get swamped in.

"You can do this, Codie Ray. You have to do this."

Solidified by hearing those words spoken out loud, I take that final step to the door. Unlocking the three deadbolts and the chain, I take a deep breath, close my eyes, turn the handle, and pull.

One, two, three...

Ryder

Heal. Recover. Trauma.

Three fucking words I'm so sick of that if I hear them said one more time, I *am* going to go just as postal as my team thinks I'm headed.

I'm just fucking fine.

What I need is to get back in the field. To have a purpose. I'm fucking sick to death of sitting on my ass and doing jack shit but workouts. It's been nearly three years since my capture and subsequent torture, and two years since I was rescued by my team after being left for dead in a cave deep in the desert. If not for some local tribe leader and his son coming upon my body and making a call to the United States government, I'd be dead for sure. Just like my captors wanted. The whole ordeal was nothing but pain and torment. I barely remember where we were sequestered, how often we moved, or what they wanted.

While the Syrians that took me knew how to put a man through his paces, they hadn't broken me. That much I do know. It's why my back, chest, and arms are covered in scars. They put China's torture of a thousand cuts to shame.

I suffered a year in hell before my team found me then spent another year in rehab and psychiatric hell before I was released into the real world again. It took six months more before I was finally able to reconnect with my family in Loveland, Colorado. Hayes, my sister, found herself a good man, a fighter with a mean upper cut. Levi takes care of her, and that's all I gave a shit about.

On my return home, she was pissed at me. Pissed

that I left and led her to believe I was dead. That wasn't quite my fault, however. But I get her anger. The night my parents were notified of my disappearance, my baby sister lost everything, too. Nearly, her life. Her Olympic dreams were crushed in a second.

She'll never find out that I paid those punk ass shits a visit, or that Foster had some fun explaining all the ways he could thread an explosive through their dicks.

After spending a few months at home with my family, I packed up to join my team in West Virginia. While we live a high-action career, we all like the sedate town of Charleston. It isn't overly small, but it isn't bustling like a major city either. We're able to relax and unwind after a long mission.

Which brings me to today. I run...every day. Same time, same pace, same route. Being in my line of work, you'd think I wouldn't, but the routine helps me shake off the demons chasing me. Lately, the past week or so, the girl next door—the one who never goes outside, whose windows are always closed, and I don't think I've seen a visitor outside of delivery vehicles—has been sitting in her doorway.

She watches me. Even when she tries not to, I catch her. Her gaze follows me with an emotion I can't quite identify. She always appears sad when I pass her house. I'm not even sure she knows that I'm her neighbor and not just some random guy from the block.

Feeling her gaze on me again has me wondering who she is. So, after a quick shower, I run a search through the city's housing database and find out her name is Codie Ray. She's the only person listed on the mortgage. For twenty years old, I'm impressed. She owns her own home. Not many people her age can afford that.

Curiosity highly piqued, I do a few more searches on her. She pays for nearly everything to be delivered; lots of online shopping. No car listed with the DMV. Nothing obvious to show if she has a significant other or not, but from what I can tell, she doesn't leave her home. Even her job, a merchant dealer online, she can do from home.

"I wonder what her damage is."

There has to be something wrong with Codie. No twenty-year-old girl stays home as much as she does without reason. I'm tempted to hack into her medical files but figure that's a hit on her privacy even I can't take.

When I joined Task Force 779, I knew I was going to be violating a lot of laws, people's privacy, and countless other scenarios. I knew there would be nothing left untouched when it came to our missions. It was my job to know everything, to make sure my team didn't go in blind. Not researching everything there is to know about my mysterious neighbor is a punch to the gut.

She's been here longer than I have from what I can tell, but until a week ago, I don't ever remember seeing her. I've never paid this much attention before, either. But now that I know she's here, I can't stop thinking about her.

CHAPTER 2
Coolie

It worked. Good lord did it work. I opened the door that first day, and while it was overwhelming and I barely lasted a minute, it was freeing to have that power.

I knew I could close the door at any time, and when I did, I'd be able to open it again. After three weeks of repeating that action, once a day for a few minutes, I've gained a small amount of control over my life again. My fears don't run this for me.

I do.

I've timed it so that when I've got deliveries coming, I'll be sitting on the floor, waiting, sketching with the door wide open.

Today, I'm waiting for a different reason. There's this man, and at the same time every day, he runs past my house at a steady pace. He's the first guy to make me feel like a woman in far longer than I care to admit. He's the first person I've looked at with anything other than repulsion in over two years.

He appears so powerful, like a soldier out to save the world. A grim expression usually covers his handsome features. I can't see much from my perch, but his jaw is strong, solid, and his eyes are always focused in front of him. I doubt he even knows I watch as he passes by.

Recognizing the padding of his feet just seconds before he appears, my sole focus is on him. "One. Two. Three." I count his steps. "One. Two. Three." I'm not OCD. I just like small numbers. It gives me a sense of calm. "One. Two. Three." And he's gone. Two neighbors down and I won't see him again until this time tomorrow. I don't even know where he lives.

Picking up my stuff, I'm about to close the door when I pause as I see a sedan driving slowly down the block. The windows are tinted so I can't see the occupants, and they don't stop in front of anyone's house or even hesitate as they pass a certain address. I don't know who they are or what they want, but I don't like it.

I can identify everyone's vehicles on the block, and this one is out of place. I close the door, counting the deadbolts as I lock them. "One, two, three." Feeling calmer, but I still watch through the peephole until the car has left my sight.

For the rest of the day, that strange vehicle is all I can seem to think about as I fill purchases for the online retailer I work for. I distribute money and orders to various companies, and normally, it's only a few hours out of my day to process, but because I can't concentrate worth crap, it takes me longer than anticipated.

Making myself a quick fruit salad for a late dinner, I finally sit down to watch the first night of Shark Week. Disappointment slams me when I hit the power button on the remote and nothing happens. The TV turns on, but the cable box remains blank.

Seeing how late it is, I know I won't reach the cable company today, so I opt for bed instead and hope to get some sleep. Tomorrow, I promise myself, I'll try and step out onto the porch for a full minute.

I miss the feeling of thick grass between my toes, and by the summer's end, that's my goal. To touch the grass again.

Sleep claims me quickly, so when I'm awoken suddenly, my entire body tenses as I try to listen for what disturbed the quiet night. Surrounded by stretched silence, I wait as my erratic heartbeat drowns out any noise and evens out. Not noticing any out of place sounds, I ever so slowly crack open my eyelids.

A lone figure stands facing the window that is above my dresser on the opposite wall, and I fight not to scream, jerk around in my bed, or run. I struggle to remain perfectly still. I battle to control the increased breathing from my lungs.

Remembering my cell phone is on my nightstand, I creep my hand forward, careful not to make any noise or moves that will draw the intruder's attention from whatever he's doing. With a firm grip, I strain not to pull my arm too quickly back under the covers where I can, hopefully, hide the light from the phone display.

Switching the mute button on, I dial 911 and let it ring long enough that someone picks up and says hello twice. Hanging up, I pray that the movies and news stories are right, and the operators are required to call back.

I wait with bated breath just as the phone rings silently in my hand. As I accept the call, the mysterious person turns around. I glide the phone under my pillow, hitting "end call" as I do, and I pray he doesn't realize what I've done.

Pushing the phone so it's squished under my head, I move my hand forward subtly and force myself not to tense at his approach to the side of the bed. Closing my eyes, I do my best to relax my facial muscles and hide the whimper trying to break free.

I've never been so vulnerable before, and I scarcely

know what to do when I feel the man's shadow tower over me, encompassing me in his evil presence. The waiting is the worst. I'm terrified he'll touch me, and I won't be able to contain my terror.

Relief nearly has me sighing out a deep breath when I hear sirens in the distance coming closer. My call worked!

The person's footsteps are heavy as they retreat down the hallway. I don't hear a door open or shut, and I can only hope he's left quietly and isn't waiting to see if I come downstairs.

I'm paralyzed with fear even as I see lights flashing in the window and hear banging on the door. I just can't move. I don't want to move. I want to wake up and for this to have been just a nightmare. I want to believe there wasn't some intruder in my home, my sanctuary.

"Miss Ray!" A voice yells from outside. "I need you to come to the door, or we'll be breaking it down!"

More intrusion?

That gets me out of bed faster than anything else could have.

Wrapping my quilt tightly around my body, I rush down the stairs in the hopes I don't trip and fall as my feet move faster than my brain can process right now.

"Miss Ray!" Pounding follows the yelling.

"One, two, three." I flick the deadbolts quickly. Peaking around the door, I whisper, "Hi."

"Miss Codie Ray?" one uniformed officer asks with a firm tone.

"That's me." My voice squeaks like a mouse.

"You made a call to 911. Is anything amiss?" His tone gentles.

Swallowing around the nervous lump in my throat, I croak out, "Someone was here, in my bedroom."

The officer and the other two men around him stand straighter. "Can we come in, take a look around?"

Pushing the door wider, I have to control the urge to shut them out. I don't like new people in my home, but I need them right now.

"Miss, if you'll follow me out to the cruiser to wait…" The first officer expects me to go with him. He doesn't know that I'm so messed up that I can't leave my home. He doesn't know my agoraphobia cripples me with fear every moment of every day.

"I can't," I whisper and wait for the judgment to enter their stern gazes.

Ryder

"You really think you're ready to come back, Tac? Full-time." Nix, my team leader, asks me. His leveled stare pulls no bullshit as our eyes meet.

"Been ready for a long time, Knot." With my elbows on my knees, I pull on the label of my beer as I await not only my boss', but longtime friend's, answer.

Task Force 779 isn't just an unstoppable team. We aren't just men with low morals—or high, depending on how you looked at it. We're family. They're my brothers. I have their backs, and they have mine. Always.

"I want you back, Ryder. Hell, we all do." He takes a long pull of the beer in his hand. "I know you have nightmares. I know you're still struggling."

Holding back my anger and resentment takes everything I have. "I lost more than my freedom that day, Nix." I can feel his stare as I speak. "I lost more than my mind in that cave."

"I fucking know, Ry. We all do. When we found you...Fuck!" He drags a hand down his face. "I didn't think you'd pull through."

"I'm ready." I have nothing else to fucking say. It's been two years, and I'm fucking ready. "I want my life back!" My words are harsh but steady.

"Alright." The look in his steely gaze says he's not quite convinced. "I want you to do an easy one. In and out and we're done."

"Deal. When do we leave?" I'm so fucking eager to get back in the field that I'll take anything at this point.

Shaking his head, he says, "Three days."

"What's the mission?" I don't really care what it is.

"Escorting the U.S. Ambassador back into Moldova. Russia isn't too happy about Turkey supporting them with their agreement to withdraw the Russian troops, so things have become dicey."

"We drop and run? Protection detail?" Interesting, but not unheard of for us.

"It's the President's cousin." And now it makes more sense.

"Whatever floats their boat, man."

Before we can further discuss the assignment, sirens blare outside my front door, and lights flash as multiple cars come to a stop.

"What the hell?" For two in the morning, it's a lot of commotion.

"I thought you said this was a quiet street?" Nix smirks.

"It is." Stepping outside, I see two cruisers parked sideways on the street and three officers running for my cute neighbor's door. "Shit," I mutter, running outside barefoot.

"Always sticking your nose in shit." Nix laughs at me from the porch.

"Codie!" I call, giving away my curiosity about the

woman. As I round the corner of her garage, I see one officer with his hand on her elbow trying in vain to get her to follow him.

Her eyes laser into me as they both notice I'm walking closer. "Sir, you can't be here," the officer says. Ignoring him, all of my focus is on Codie. The fear in her eyes. The trembling in her slight body.

"She's fucking terrified," I snap at the cop, who finally lets her go to walk towards me.

"You need to leave. We're checking for an intruder." I attempt to walk past him when he places a hand on my chest. "I said, you need to leave!"

I stop, if only to quell the worry in Codie's tear-filled eyes. "Are you okay?" I ask her, still ignoring the man with his hand on my chest.

"Let him go," Nix snaps behind me, flashing a badge the whole team was given when we were recruited. "Presidential detail." It's not a complete lie, but it's the one we tell when asked.

"What the hell does that have to do with her?" The cop is rightfully confused by Nix's words, but he lets me go, so I don't give a shit.

"Not a lot. But he's not going to fuck shit up for you. Just wants to support the girl." I drown out the rest of what they say as I stand just a few feet from Codie.

"What happened?" I ask her.

She seems unsure. Her feet shift from side to side,

and she looks like she wants to run but can't. Her stare keeps straying to the front lawn. Confused, I look around and see nothing out of the ordinary.

"Codie?" My voice is firmer in the hopes that she'll answer me.

When her light green eyes snap to mine, I hold my breath. They sear me to my core. Take hold of my heart and refuse to let go. "How do you know my name?" Her voice is soft, skeptical. Smart girl.

Smirking, I tell her honestly. "You've been watching me." Her blush gives her fair skin some color. "I've been watching you, too." And she pales again.

"So, you know then?" Her question doesn't make sense. Neither does the shame in her voice.

"Know what?" I ask, but she doesn't get to answer.

"House is all clear!" One cop calls out as he descends the stairs from the second floor of her house. "Who are you?"

"Ryder Morrison," I tell him. I can feel Nix's imposing frame walk up behind me.

"Nix Bishop, Presidential detail."

"Why are you here?" The third cop asks.

"Just being neighborly," I respond because, what else can I say? That I've slowly become enthralled with my neighbor? That I've done all kinds of research on her and still can't figure her out? That doesn't sound creepy at all.

"Right." All three officers ignore us as they face Codie again. "Ma'am, the house is empty. Whoever was here is long gone now."

"An intruder? Did he hurt you?" Pushing my way in front of her, I search her delicate frame for obvious injuries.

"I'm fine," she whispers, and her confusion is back.

"If you could come–"

"No!" she snaps, stepping back from everyone, poised to run at any second.

"Ma'am, we need–"

"I said, no."

"You called us, miss. We can't help if we don't have details." The first officer is annoyed and letting it bleed through his words.

"I can't tell you anything. My room is dark. Something woke me up. The man was standing in front of my window, or I never would have seen him. I don't know how tall he was, if he had distinguishing marks, nothing. It was dark." I can hear her voice shaking as the officers try to box her in.

Stepping in the middle, I turn my back to them, ignoring their presence as I grip Codie's shoulders. Her tensing doesn't stop me from rubbing circles with my thumbs. "Breathe," I encourage.

"How do you know my name?" she asks again.

"You watched me for weeks, Codie. I was curious." I have no shame.

"If you're not going to make a statement, miss, we have another call."

"What the fuck is wrong with you? You can't take her goddamned statement here? She's fucking terrified." I've lost my temper, and I see Nix glaring at me, but I don't care.

Codie

I'm sure I look every bit as stupefied as I feel gazing up at this strange man. The one I've watched run past my house for weeks. I don't understand how or why he's here. I don't understand anything right now.

"Ryder," his friend barks, drawing everyone's attention. "Leave it alone."

"Fuck off, Nix. I'm not on Sam's dime right now," my hero bites back.

"Miss, do you care to make a statement?" one of the officers asks again. They want me to go to the station. To leave my home. I can't. As much as I want to step outside this door... I just can't.

His—Ryder's—hands on my shoulders are comforting as I try to do what needs to be done. "I have nothing to add other than what I told you already. If you want me to sign something, fine, but I can't leave." I feel the dozen questions in his gaze.

The judgment in the others'.

It's always the same. Everyone thinks I'm a freak. Weird. Not right in the head.

Maybe they're right. Maybe there is something wrong with me. No, not maybe, I *know* there is. I'm ten thousand shades of screwed up. I have been for over two years now, and after tonight, I'm not sure I want that to change.

Except it might have to.

"How did he get in?" No one has keys to my house. I keep my doors and windows locked at all times. It's not possible. *Did I imagine it?*

A shared look goes around the room, and I know exactly what they're all thinking.

"Get out," I hiss.

I didn't make this up dammit.

"Ma'am, have you been drinking this evening?" The rude officer asks.

I stare. Completely dumbfounded. I don't even know how to answer a question like that without slapping him across the face. "No." I grit my teeth. "I don't drink."

"Drugs?"

Shaking my head, I fight the anger and fear burning me up inside. "No."

"Look, if something happened, we need to know what you were on."

"Her fucking pupils are fine. She isn't slurring her words, and she's not falling over drunk," Ryder's friend snaps. "Do your fucking jobs and find out how he got in!" The command in the man's voice has all three officers standing taller.

"There was no forced entry. No marks on windows or door locks. The only conclusion is that someone had a key." They all look to me.

"I'm the only person with any keys."

"Have you ever left them unattended?" Ryder inquires.

"No." I bite down my embarrassment. I hate my situation. The dark fears living in the back of my mind.

"Anyone been over recently?" his friend asks patiently.

I shake my head.

"Then I'm sorry, ma'am, but we don't have much to go on," the quietest officer says, sincere regret in his eyes.

"Thank you for coming out. Maybe I was wrong, and a shadow was playing on the walls or something."

Except it wasn't. But I'm dealing with men who only operate in cold hard facts. Of which I have none.

Ryder's friend escorts the officers to their cruisers while I fight back my tears and wonder why he's still standing in my doorway.

I refuse to break first. I don't know this man. I might have admired his sexy physique for weeks, but I don't know him from Adam, and he doesn't know me.

"What did you mean when you said I knew?" He breaks the silence while his eyes roam the inside of my house. My now shattered haven.

"Nothing." I don't want to get into this right now.

"Liar." Our eyes clash, and I'm actually shocked that he's calling me on my bullshit.

"Look, Mr. Morrison, it's late. I'm tired. While I appreciate you coming over to check on me, I'd like you to leave now. Please."

"That hurt, didn't it?" He smirks like something's funny.

"What hurt?"

"Saying please."

As Ryder walks away, I don't know whether to be insulted by his remark or laugh. He can't understand how hard it is to have so many strangers in my house at one time. He'll never know just how disjointed I am on the inside.

My fears run deeper than a black hole. Losing Lucas

is the worst kind of pain a person can feel. Knowing how precious life is, how quickly it can be taken away, started me on a downward spiral that I haven't been able to crawl out of.

After I was able to open my eyes from the grief, every fear I've ever had came flying to the surface and soon, I became afraid of my own shadow. It's how I ended up where I am now. How I am now.

It's still dark outside, the middle of the night, and I don't know how the hell I'm supposed to function in this house now that it's been violated. I can no longer call it a safe place...my sanctuary. This house no longer holds the same meaning it used to.

Closing the door behind me, I count, "One, two, three," as I turn the deadbolts one at a time. It helps soothe some of my anxiety but not much. I need more. I need comfort.

I need not be so damn broken.

Walking through the house, I do as one of the policemen had just done and make sure all the windows are locked as I turn on every overhead light and lamp I have. No shadows, no weird noises. No hiding. If he comes back, I'll be ready.

Ryder

I listened as she locked her door, counted out loud with the click of each bolt, before leaving. I watched while walking back to my house as her lights turned on one by one, and I bet they won't be going out anytime soon.

Nix is standing by his truck as I approach, shaking his head. "You want back on the team, you get your head in the game, Morrison." The man is a hard son of a bitch, and he has to be for what we do. Doesn't mean I want his shit right now.

"It is."

"Not with her, it isn't. She's fucked up. She'll get you killed quicker than a grenade."

"I said I'm fine, Nix. Leave it the fuck alone."

"Whatever, kid, but if you're distracted, I'm pulling you without remorse. I won't let some silly girl scared of her own shadow get my men killed, you got that?"

Ignoring him, I walk away. I've lived through enough shit to last me a lifetime. They can't even fucking comprehend. Nix doesn't fucking know just how much I went through before coming home. My pretty little neighbor certainly isn't going to fuck my life up because I'm concerned.

Slamming my front door shut behind me, I jog up the stairs to my room. Stripping free of my shorts and shirt, I stand in front of the mirror, eyeing the damage done to me, facing the truth of where my hell took me. The guys think this was all my captors. They'd be ashamed to know the scars on my forearms are from me. They'd be astonished to know that after six months in hell, I gave up. I was ready to be done with the sheer agony brought on me day after day for information I wasn't willing to give. Some of which, I didn't even have.

They'd likely skin me alive if they knew that not only had I tried taking my own life, I failed in stopping another captive from successfully snuffing out his own. I handed him the glass I'd found and watched as he slit his throat, blood spurting across the walls of our caged cave. We had no reason to believe anyone was coming for us. I was an American on soil I wasn't authorized to be on. He was a Brit in foreign territory when his troops were ambushed and killed. The single survivor. No one even knew he was still there.

What hope did we have other than a quick death?

The one thing we did do was tell each other our names and unit numbers. He was British intelligence. Like me, working a clandestine mission for Scotland Yard. It took three months after I had recovered enough to remember all that happened, and I was able to tell his commanding officer what had happened to him.

My chest is littered with scars from being their

whipping boy. They used to make a game of torturing me. I don't know when, but they realized I wasn't going to talk, so I became their entertainment while they waited for their orders.

When my team found me, when they came barrelassing into that fucking cave, I thought I had to have been hallucinating. I didn't believe they were real. I actually hit Theo, my best friend, so hard in the face that I fractured his nose. When they started talking about Hayes, I broke. They knew she was the only thing in the world to bring me back from the edge. Foster had the picture of her I kept in my locker at headquarters. They knew they were coming for me, and they showed up prepared.

Understanding how pissed she still is at me, even though she welcomes me home with open arms each time, it fucking kills me. More than any of these scars, the nightmares, anything. I get her anger, though, and I think there's more to it than just me taking so long to get in contact after I was found. She gets recovery better than most would. After all she's been through, I'll take her anger over silence.

Turning to the shower, I get it as warm as I can stand before dipping into the scalding water. Thoughts of Codie linger in my mind, and while I don't know her or what she meant by her cryptic comment, I acknowledge that I want to learn more about her.

As skittish as she is, as defeated as she seems, I realize she's going to mean something to me, and the more I think about it, the more I admit that I want her to mean something to me, too. I want her to be more than my fucked-up neighbor.

Getting through the shower quickly, I'm drying off when I hear loud thumping coming from my neighbor's house. Looking out my window, I notice her in a room across from mine, lights blazing as she puts up a sheet of wood over the window. She's boarding herself inside.

Confused doesn't begin to describe how she makes me feel. Seeing that the time is after three in the morning, I know I need to get some shut-eye before I head down to headquarters and check my gear for this mission that we leave on in three days. I want to show Nix and the guys I'm ready to come back. I want to prove to Nix that Codie hasn't fucked my mind six ways from Sunday, and she's not a distraction.

CHAPTER 3
Ryder

*A*fter listening to Codie pound the night away, I'm up and leaving as dawn pushes the horizon into a mix of pinks, purples, and reds. I give her house one last look as I back my Toyota Tacoma out of the driveway and shake my head. Seeing that all her front windows are boarded up, as well, worries me.

The drive to Charleston's warehouse district isn't a long one, so I don't get much time to think about my quirky neighbor before I'm exiting into one of the quietest parts of the city.

Observing the building from the outside, you'd never know it was a full tactical command center equipped with a massive gym, training center, and a vault filled with an intimidating weapons arsenal.

Anything we could ever need is here, and anything we don't have is one presidential call away.

With underground parking, it's never revealed who is here until we pass through the facial scan and into the garage. Stealing myself for my first look into the newly renovated facility, I hold my breath as the bay door opens and lights flood the area in front of me.

Seeing Theo's bike and Foster's sports car, I feel relief that I won't be facing the space empty and alone. After parking, I exit my truck and walk the short way to the elevator. As soon as the doors close, I step towards the wall panel for the retina scan. Theo used to joke that this place was tighter than the White House with security.

After everything that's happened to me, I can't laugh him off anymore. If the world comes under attack, this is the place I'd want to be.

The ascent to the main floor is quick, and as soon as the doors open, I hear the ruckus that is Foster and Theo as they play a game of pool in the main room. The most competitive bastards on the team, these games usually end in a brawl on the floor with the accusations of cheating from both.

They stop, and quiet descends as soon as they see me. A huge grin takes over Theo's face as he walks forward. "Ryder! My man, good to see back here." A hard clap on the back nearly knocks the breath from me. At just over six feet tall, Theo is large with the strength to match. His Greek ancestry shows through with his dark looks, too. People always think of him as intense because of it, along with the tattoos covering the majority of his body. Not really knowing him, they'd never expect he was one of the funniest—if not most morally corrupt—guys I know.

"Good to be back, man." My eyes search the warehouse, assessing, regaining my familiarity for the changes as Foster comes forward and brings me in for a rough hug.

"Fucking good to see you here, bro." His typically rough voice sounds slightly emotional, which doesn't shock me. He's always been the sensitive one of the team, even though he's a complete psycho with explosives.

"Thanks, Chaos." He earned the nickname after his first mission on the team. Nix asked him for a distraction as they were extracting some CEO from a hostage situation in Vietnam. This was before my time. He set a small explosion next to what he thought was cold food storage in the terrorist's camp, but it turned out to be their own explosives shed. From the way they tell it, there's likely still a hole big enough to fit three tankers.

Walking around the room, I get a feel again for the building that had become my life for so many years. Before being captured, I anticipated the next mission, needing them one after another. They were an addiction. I craved the adrenaline rush as much as the next guy. I felt invincible.

Until Syria.

Until I wasn't.

"You okay, man?" Phantom asks. Theo is the one you never see coming. Top of his class in marksmanship, he's a high valued asset for the United States government. He watches me now with assessing eyes as I wander around. "You ready to be back?"

"Yeah, I'm ready." I may be finding my footing again, but I'm fucking raring to go. If being captured, and subsequently tortured, has taught me one thing, it's that this world needs to be rid of these sons of bitches sooner rather than later.

"Good. I want you on the targets with Phantom." I hear Nix speak from behind me, and I turn. His glare is cold. Everything about the man is stoic. Not many know that Nix 'Knot' Bishop hides his caring disposition behind the icy stares, though.

"You got it, boss." I give him a mock salute as Theo nearly busts a gut laughing at the look on his face. "I see your sense of humor hasn't made an appearance yet." He never did get a joke.

"Nothing funny about knowing the men behind me have my back," Nix states. Point made.

"Come on, man, before that vein in his neck bursts

from the need to kill one of us." Theo laughs as he walks away and into the hallway leading to the ammunitions bay.

As I stroll the building, I notice the little things that have changed while I've been gone. It's subtle to a civilian's gaze, but I see it. More security cameras in the corners. Thumbprint scanner to get through any doors other than storage and bathrooms. Even the locker room has one.

"Theo, what's with all the extra security? We have a breach I don't know about?" I'm only half kidding, but it's always a possibility.

"Nah, Shaker got antsy when you were brought back. Put his time and frustration to good use around here." Weston Green is our team medic and earned the name Shaker as a joke when he was in the Army because he never shakes with nerves. Always has a steady hand.

"So, it's not needed then?"

"Not really, no. Knot thought it was a good idea afterwards, though, so he hasn't complained. Much."

After pressing a thumb to the fingerprint scanner, the door slides open and, first, reveals the ammunitions locker. Handguns line the wall in front of me with the automatic weapons to my left. An island sits in the middle of the room with drawers filled to capacity with different types of combat knives.

The wall on the right holds bulletproof vests, bags to store the weapons in, backpacks and straps to put whatever accessories we want on our bodies.

A secret door is hidden between the handguns and the storage wall leading to the target range running 100 meters out. Grabbing my favorite Berretta and protective gear, I head out. We have a bigger one on a piece of property where we plan missions and fly out with a helicopter, but this location is used mostly for training and strategy practice.

Hanging a target, I wait until Theo is lined up next to me before I hit the go button beside me. Lights flash, and our paper targets are sent to the back of the room.

"Ready?" Phantom grins at me. The asshole knows he's a better shot than I am, and he'll take whatever chance he can to gloat.

Nodding, the sound of gunfire echoes around the room. Odd as it may be, it's a soothing sound to me. Concentration is easier, and I find myself getting back into the groove of hitting center mass targets.

All too soon my chamber is empty, and the click of a useless trigger registers to my ears. With images of the men who captured me, I hit the button to bring my paper forward.

"Hot damn!" Theo cheers beside me. Looking to his target, I expect to see him pulling some sort of stunt and making an image with the bullets. He's done it before. His artistic talent, he says. "I don't think you've ever beat me, Tac."

"What?" I look to the silhouette as it stops in front of my face, and sure enough, a cluster of holes sits in one spot. Center mass. Right on target. I'm not saying I'm a lousy shot, but I'm not on par with Theo, or even Nix. My expertise is technology. "Damn," I mutter, pulling the paper down and staring.

"Looks like you've got a new muse, Morrison," Nix says, coming up beside me. "I'm impressed."

Nix? Impressed? Fuck. Shrugging, I say to him, "I've been on the range a lot lately."

"I know. Camden has kept me in the loop." Camden is a man who runs the metro police open range. He allows us to come in as often as we need. For the past eight months, I've been going in weekly.

Patting my shoulder, Nix leaves Theo and me again.

"Alright, hotshot, let's try my baby this time. See if you outdo me again." As disgruntled as he's trying to act, I can tell he's happy I'm back and better than ever before.

"Twenty minutes, guys!" Foster's voice comes through the speaker.

Grabbing Theo's gun of choice—an M17 Pistol—we make our way through three more targets each, with me keeping up with him every step of the way.

I guess if one good thing could come from my

capture, it's that I can finally gloat in Theo's face about my newfound skills.

Codie

Learning who my mysterious runner is now, I realize that Ryder lives next door to me. I saw that he left early this morning and even as the sun begins to set, I know he's not home yet.

After boarding up my house, I spent all day in front of my computer pounding out three days of work so I could remain distracted.

Fear paralyzes me as my eyes burn, and my mind begs for sleep. I can't, though. If I close my eyes, whoever broke in could come back, and I'd be more vulnerable than before because now he knows that I know he was here.

I spent some time today trying to figure out what could have happened, how he got in, who he was. The sedan from yesterday kept popping into my mind, but even that didn't make sense because I haven't seen it since then, and I don't recall noticing it when the police arrived last night.

Maybe they are right; I am losing my mind.

I wanted to believe I could get past my illness. I wanted to believe I could have a life. But what if all I'm meant for is to be lonely? An outsider forever looking in.

CHAPTER 4
Codie

oom. Crash. Bang.

I flinch with each noise. Cry out every time the thunder sounds.

After boarding up every window in the house two days ago, I moved myself into the small den off the front door. With a quick shot to the kitchen and a rounded corner to the bathroom, I don't need to be anywhere else in my house.

I haven't opened my door since Ryder left, and I've become even more sheltered. The mere thought of opening it wide when I have supplies being delivered tomorrow throws me into a deep panic.

I'm fuming mad at myself, too. I was getting better. I was making progress, and one stupid shadow scares me into becoming this...this...I don't even know what I am anymore. I hate it. I hate myself for what I've allowed myself to become. This isn't the life I was supposed to have. This is someone else's. I keep telling myself that I almost feel a little better. Then I remember the fear. It hits me out of nowhere. This suffocating loneliness wraps around me like a tidal wave.

I'm more convinced now than when the officers suggested it that it was my imagination wreaking havoc with my mind. Nobody was here, there was no way for them to get in. I made whoever it is up. It's a demon in my mind that needs to be forced back into my subconscious so I can breathe again.

I want to be better. I want to go out. I want to live without fear. But I'm terrified it's never going to be me. I'll live in this depressing hole until I'm dead, until I've been hiding for so long that no one even remembers I exist. I'll let all the good things a person has in life pass me by because I can't get out of my own fucking head!

I don't want to be like this. I would hate to miss out on life, but I don't see any other options. I've tried to work my way out of this; I've tried for so long and so hard to move past my fears. I was almost there this time.

Ryder had been a weird part of it, too. His routine of running past my house, it was something to look forward to. A beacon of light on my gloomy days.

Until he met me. Now, I'm this strange girl next

door who watches him, and he doesn't run anymore. At least, not past my house. I haven't seen him since locking my doors that night.

Part of me is sad about that because when he touched me, spoke to me like a real person and not some freak of nature, I felt something. I don't understand what it was, but it was there, and it was tangible. I could have held onto it if only I saw him again.

Now, I'm left to wonder if he wasn't a figment of my imagination, as well.

Boom. Crash. Bang.

I flinch with each noise. Hide deeper in the stupid little fort I've made between the couch and two end tables. I'm five again and hiding from thunderstorms, only I don't have Abby, my childhood dog, to keep me safe from the monsters in my closet.

Boom. Crash. Bang.

When will this nightmare end?

Ryder

"Comms check." I tap the mic in my ear as I watch

through a camera drone that I'm flying over the team from a location eight miles away.

"Check," Knot grumbles through the line as he stands guard outside the helicopter that just landed with the ambassador in it.

"Check," Shaker says from his position inside the building, securing any unexpected visitors as they enter. The embassy has more people coming and going than a fucking whorehouse at dawn.

"Check." I see Chaos shake his head from the ground, pushing any lingering vehicles along with threats of a bullet to the brain or prison in an unstable country of his choosing. It might not be legal, but it gets people moving.

"You know you're becoming obsessed with this shit, right?" Phantom laughs through the line. His perch four buildings south of the embassy gives him a hawk's-eye view of all of us, and anyone else who might have a fancy to take out one of the few people trying to bring stability to the country. "Christ sake, check." His curse keeps going, but he knows I won't say a word until I hear a response from each of them.

"Better safe than sorry." I can see Nix tense at my words, and I know what's going through his head. He thinks I'm not ready. Well, I am. I'm just more cautious than I used to be. "Heads up, Chaos, tour truck coming your way from the east. Backs loaded down. No tourists visible in the windows." Why they'd need a tour truck is beyond me. Moldova is not anyone's vacation destination.

"Got it. Phantom, you got the driver?"

"In my sight."

"Something's going on in here, guys. People are running scared," Shaker reports back.

"Use caution," Knot commands just as the truck stops.

"Tac, you scanning this thing? Driver won't look at me."

Studying the thermal images, I switch to x-ray and see an empty truck. Gotta love Uncle Sam's high-tech gadgets. "It's empty," I relay but begin scanning farther out as Nix escorts the ambassador off the chopper.

"Something's not right." Chaos echoes my thoughts. "Phantom, you see anything?"

"Negative. No active combatants." As soon as he says the words, I hear the hum of a drone directly above me.

"Fuck."

"What?" Nix snaps as he hands the ambassador off to Shaker inside the building. "What do you see, Tac?"

"Drone, directly overhead of me." Without knowing if they realize I'm here, I can only assume it's the Russians trying to surveil what the fuck is going on. They won't know it's American government operatives doing the escorting today because we don't wear colors or flags—black or green all the way. They will likely assume, however.

"Weaponized or overwatch?" Phantom asks. "I've got it in my sights."

Gazing up, I use my binoculars for a clearer view. "Overwatch," I comment back. It's similar to my own model.

"Security's here," Chaos reports. That's our cue to leave. "They've got the driver in custody. No bomb on the truck."

"Report back to the rendezvous point ASAP," Knot snaps.

I watch as all the members of my team pack up before grabbing my own gear and starting the mile-long trek to where our pick-up is located. "Tac, get your ass in gear. We have ten minutes," Theo snaps, and I understand his worry. Last time I was getting ready to meet them, I never made it.

This time will be different. I'll be there. But before I go, I pull out a small camera from my pack and take pictures of the drone still hovering above my position. I get a dozen shots off before darting into the clearing beyond the woods behind me.

Hearing the sounds of blades whooshing through the air, I break free of the tree line in time to see our chopper landing. As we load into the beast of a machine, a dove—yeah, the bird—takes flight alongside us and even though I'm baffled as to its place here, it reminds me of Codie back home.

For the first time since becoming airborne less than twenty-four hours ago, she's on my mind. The dove, fragile, pure, in need of protection, reminds me so much of my own little dove.

As the guys break down the mission in-flight, all I can think about is returning home. Seeing Codie. Holding her in my arms. Wondering if she's still got the boards up over her windows. I silently compel our pilot to move faster. Knowing without seeing, that she's sheltering herself away. That she's trapped in whatever hell is holding her prisoner.

CHAPTER 5
Codie

*I*t's been quiet, too quiet, for days. I can't think straight. I haven't eaten. Breathing is difficult, and I can't move. I've been in this damn panicked state for two days straight, and no matter how hard I try, I can't get my head on right.

I complained about being weird and isolated, hated the way I couldn't break out of my shell before, now, I just wish for the me of a week ago. I wish I were opening my front door and feeling the cool breeze on my flesh. Hearing the sounds of the people in my neighborhood as they went about their busy days.

I want to be me again. Whether the normal or fucked up one, I don't care, I just hate this defeated girl I've turned into. I hate how broken I've become in such a short time.

I had dreams once. I wanted to travel the world. Visit Sicily, Rome, Paris. I wanted to immerse myself in another country's culture. To explore the ruins of Peru, travel by boat along the Amazon in Brazil. I longed to see Mount Everest if only to say I'd been there. To see the pyramids in Egypt. Learn about ancient castles in Ireland.

Instead, I'm stuck here, hiding in a home that feels more like a mortuary because I can't fight my demons. The world has become too much for me to handle, and with no one to help ease my pain, I'm an even more reclusive hermit who's afraid of her own shadow.

Peeking my head out of my little fort, I see daylight beginning to stream through a crack on the board over the window. When a shadow passes by the small opening, I cower in the corner. Terror paralyzes me as the sound of pounding starts on the door. I cover my ears with my hands and rock slightly. *Go away, go away, go away.* I repeat the words in my head, but the noise only intensifies.

"Codie!" I hear my name being called, but I don't recognize the voice. "Come on, dove, it's Ryder Morrison. Open the door." With my knees tight to my chest, I try desperately to move. I don't know the man well, but I trust him. When he came by the other day, he had this protective way about him that couldn't be denied.

I want to let him in, I really do, but I can't for the life of me make my body move. "Move!" I cry out.

"Codie, if you don't open this door, I'm breaking a window!" They're all covered, I don't know how he could. "Come on, Codie, I don't want to scare you any more than I'm sure you are."

I'm trying; I swear I am. But the fear has me paralyzed. I can't get my limbs or even my voice to cooperate. Tears form in my eyes, and I wipe them away angrily. I hate myself so much in this moment.

"I'm not going away, dove." His voice has softened. "I'll wait for as long as it takes. Just…let me know you're alright. Make a noise. Something, anything."

Noise…

My eyes roam around me in quick succession. Spying the hammer I used to board up all the windows, I grab it and toss it close to the door, so it clatters.

"I really need you to let me in. I need to see with my own eyes that you're not hurt." I don't know how long it's been since I've had someone care about me so much with knowing nothing more than my name.

"I'm okay," I croak, hoping he'll hear me.

He doesn't. "I'm going to wait here until you open this door. I'll be here, Codie." I could weep with his resolution to strengthen me. Because that's what he's doing by simply being here. It feels like he's fighting for me. Fighting to break me free of this hell I've trapped myself in.

I can hear him slide down the door. His head hits as he leans back with force. His frustration is palpable. "Ryder," I whisper. I know he won't hear it but saying his name out loud, it makes this all the more real in my mind.

Slowly lowering my legs, I gather every ounce of strength and determination I can muster, and I crawl to the door. My breath grows harsher with each movement. I can feel the terror igniting in the pits of my mind. The panic threatens to take control again.

I won't let it; I can't let it. I need to take back my life, and if I have to do it on my hands and knees, I'm damn well going to start there.

I slump against the door with a heavy thud, and his voice is so much closer. "Codie? Are you alright? I just need to hear your voice."

Lying on the floor, I place one hand to my heart—trying to calm myself—and the other to the door, searching out his energy, gathering some for support.

"I'm here," I say just above a whisper.

"Good, that's good, Dove." Relief is in his words. "Are you hurt? Do you need a doctor?"

"No!" I panic again at the idea of having to leave the house. "I'm fine. Physically."

"What do you mean physically?" I can almost hear the scowl in his voice.

"I'm okay, that's all."

"Can you open the door?"

My heart stops and black clouds my vision at the mere suggestion of opening myself to the outside world. I can't do it, not again. Not after last time. I was doing so well—or so I thought—and now, I'm a cowering wimp.

But Ryder won't understand. He doesn't know the demons I harbor.

"I can't." My voice cracks.

"Why?"

"I just can't."

"I need to come in, Codie. I need to see for myself that you're not being held against your will." Like anyone wants anything to do with me that way. I'm useless to society. It would be pointless.

"I'm not, I swear. I just can't open the door. Please don't make me explain it." I don't know how to; I've never had to explain it to anyone before.

"You have three locks, are they all locked?"

"Yes." I frown, wondering where he's going with his line of thinking.

"Can you open them?"

"No." My answer is immediate. I'm petrified to open

the door. That it'll be the same as the other night. Someone could come into my home again.

"How about just one? Unbolt just one, then you still have two locked, plus the door handle." He jiggles the lever as if to prove his point. Three locks, even if I unlock one.

Three locks.

One.

Two.

Three.

I'll still have three.

Three locks.

Ryder

Waiting with bated breath on her next move, I sigh with relief when I hear the locking mechanism sliding free of the top deadbolt. "That's good, Codie." I have my suspicions now about what's wrong with her, but I need my laptop. Only problem is I'm not willing to leave her to get it. I'm gaining her trust, and I won't lose it for a piece of technology.

I need to engage her, get her trust to blossom, so she'll let me in. It's not that I don't believe she's fine, it's that I don't think she's coping. After the break-in and the cops disbelief in her, and now, with her boarding her windows before I left and them remaining the same way after five days, I know she needs someone to put her faith in again.

"I'm sorry I was gone for so long. Business, you know." I can't come right out and tell her what happened.

"You work for the government; you don't owe me anything. We're not even friends." If I didn't hear the tinge of worry in her voice, I'd feel dismissed.

"We could be. We could be a lot more if you would just let me in." I'm not just talking about her house either. Since coming back, I've felt vaguely adrift, out of place. Nix isn't wrong when he keeps insisting that I'm not myself.

My whole life, I've wanted to do something to help humanity. I've searched for a home that wasn't my own. A place where I belong. In the Navy, I came close. In Task Force 779, I found everything I'd been searching for. Acceptance, brotherhood, friendship, family. I love my biological family. My parents have always been great, and Hayes has been my best friend, but I'm still left feeling unfilled.

"I can't be anyone's anything, Ryder." Her voice

catches on my name. "I'm so broken. More than you can ever understand."

"Broken can be fixed." I rap my knuckles on the wood beneath me in tune to my heartbeat. "I was once." I don't know how else to get to her. "Three years ago, I was captured and tortured in a foreign country." Talking about it has gotten easier over the years, but the memories still swamp me. "I didn't think I'd ever get rescued, let alone have a second chance to live my life."

"I'm so sorry." She sounds like she's crying.

"They held me for a year. I have scars, mentally and physically, that I'll carry with me for the rest of my life." When I hear a deadbolt unlock, I sit up taller. "When I saw Nix and Theo come crashing into that cave, guns at the ready, a look in their eyes saying they expected to find me dead, that was my strength to fight the rest of my way out of that cave. It gave me the power to break free of my demons."

"You're so strong," she whispers through the door. From the pitch of her voice, I think she's laying on the floor, so I lower my body.

"That day, my strength came from my team. Even though they suspected I was likely dead. In fact, they had found remains that led them to believe I *was* dead at one time. But they still investigated that one tip that hinted I was alive. I couldn't be more grateful." I won't tell her the horrors brought upon me, but I want her to know she's not alone in her turmoil. "Do you have someone to help you, Codie?"

"No." So much pain in a single syllable.

"Family, friends?"

"I'm alone."

"I have a sister. Hayes. She's been my best friend since the day she was born. And a pain in my ass just as long. When I came home last summer, she cried in my arms for nearly two days. Then she got so mad at me, she wouldn't talk to me for a few weeks."

"Why was she mad?"

My throat tightens. "I waited a year after my rescue to return home. What I went through, the humiliation and degradation I endured, it wouldn't have been right. I didn't want to bring that down on my family. I knew they would accept me no matter what, but I didn't want them to worry more than they already would.

"When I did come home, the relief was worth the wait. Because even if I wasn't completely healed, it was enough to accept their welcome. The hugs that would have made me cringe. The noises that would have made me jump. I had control over it all."

"You said a few weeks. What changed her mind?"

"Her friend needed help. Hayes is loyal to a fault, and even given the circumstances, she knew she could still trust me to help however I could. Theo, my best friend, and I went and helped her friend out of a bad situation. Hayes and I, we aren't one hundred yet, but we're getting there. Day by day."

"Are you okay now?" This woman thinks she's broken, but she isn't. She's empathetic to every human emotion, and I'm willing to bet the reason she's become so fragile is because of it.

"I am. I bear the scars of my captivity, but they've helped shape the man I've become. They've made me a better soldier."

"I want to be better, too. I want to live a real life." Her confession is filled with heartbreak. "Unfortunately, I'm not cut out for that." The sounds of movement followed by the two locks she'd unbolted being reengaged have my frustration rising.

"Dammit, Codie, you can get through this. I'm here. I'll help you." Her silence is crushing. "Codie!" I pound on the door to no avail. "Fuck!" My frustration is met with the sound of a dog howling a few doors down.

I'm not done with her yet. I won't be giving up while there's still breath left in my body.

CHAPTER 6
Ryder

"*A*re you sure about this, man?" Theo asks for the third time in as many minutes. After spending six hours sitting on Codie's front step waiting for any sign of movement, I either had to get my ass up and figure out how to help her or break the door down.

"Yeah, Theo, I'm sure." Since breaking in her door would traumatize her further, I decide a little more research is more appropriate.

"And you're sure about her diagnosis?" Despite his edgy looks with his dark hair and eyes and dozens of tattoos, Theo has a bigger heart than most men. Seeing any woman hurt and in pain can set off his trigger finger faster than someone trying to kill him.

"About ninety percent sure," I mumble in the dark as we walk up the path to her house. Pulling out the tools

I'll need to pick her locks, I knock loudly first. Even understanding that I'll startle her, I can't sit by and let her lose herself in whatever is happening. "Codie? It's Ryder. Theo's here with me. You remember I told you a bit about him?" I wait for a response I know isn't coming. "We're coming in, Codie. If you want to unlock the door, do it now; otherwise, I have the tools to do it myself." We wait a full minute before I get to work. "I'm coming in," I call to her again just in case she didn't hear me before. "Shine the light, Theo."

"Did you ever think she wasn't interested, man? Some people would call this stalking." Ignoring him, I keep going.

One deadbolt down, two to go.

Then the door handle.

"One," I hear muttered quietly from inside.

"You hear that?" Could have been my imagination.

The second lock gives. "Two."

"Is she counting?" Theo asks, leaning against the door.

"She's got a thing about threes," I tell him.

"Three? Like OCD or something?"

The third lock disengages. "Three."

Popping the door lock is easy. Entering the house, I call her name again. "Codie, it's Ryder. Theo and I are coming in."

"One, two, three." A deep breath. "One, two three." A

hiccup. "One, two, three."

"Lock the door, Theo. All three," I instruct him as I walk further into her home.

"One"—the first lock flips—"two"—the second —"three"—the final one is loud in the silent house. Darkness encompasses us as we walk into what looks to be a den. Only Codie has built herself a fortress of walls with furniture and blankets surrounding her in a small corner.

"Codie?" I call again. I need to know she hears me, knows that it's me here and not some intruder.

"The numbers, they calm me," she whispers.

"Okay." I don't care why she does it.

"I'm not obsessive."

"Whatever you say," Theo agrees.

"Check the windows, Phantom," I snap. As he walks away mumbling, I enter what seems to be her hideaway. "You okay down there?" I can see her slippered feet sticking out of a blanket.

"I guess that depends on your definition of okay." Behind her wit and sarcasm, I can hear the vulnerability she's hiding.

"Alive."

"Then, yeah, I'm unfortunately okay." I can't tell if it's sadness or relief I hear in her tone.

"Why unfortunately?"

"What are you, my shrink?"

I snort at her comment. "No. Do you have one? Should I call them?"

The blanket covering her still doesn't move. "Probably," she whispers finally poking her head out so I can see her, and what I see is not something I like.

Dark bags of exhaustion under her eyes. A paler than normal complexion. And greasy hair. It's only been five days since I've seen her, yet it looks like it's been weeks. She's a complete mess.

"When's the last time you ate?" She shrugs. "I'm gonna order some pizza. You want anything specific?" She shakes her head. After making the call for three large pizzas, she raises a brow, and I shrug, "We're growing boys."

"Why are you here, Ryder?" Her words are followed by a loud bang from upstairs. "Jesus, Theo, chill!" I call up to him. Looking back at Codie, her eyes are wild with fright, and her body is vibrating. Grabbing her ankle, I pull her out of her blankets and into my arms.

Trying to soothe her, I wrap my arms around her shaking body and whisper in her ear. "Just Theo, dove. You're fine. I won't let anything happen to you." I try to imprint my vow of safety into her, but she's skittish as a trapped rabbit. "What happened to you?"

I don't expect an answer, but the one I get saddens me immensely. "Love. Love happened."

"Tell me about it?" I want to learn about everything

there is to her. Except, I know it's not going to happen just because I want it to.

"It hurts, and hiding is easier than living."

"Do you believe in fate, Codie?" Her body is still shivering in my arms, but she's no longer tense.

"I believe that if fate is real, she's a cold-hearted bitch I want nothing to do with." The agony in her voice pulls at my heart.

"Pizza's here." Theo comes thumping down the stairs and heads for the door. As he unbolts the locks I hear, "One, two, three."

Codie

His arms feel so strong and safe wrapped around me as we sit on the floor while Theo grabs the pizza. I don't know what Ryder wants from me, but it feels a whole lot like more than I have left in me to give.

Listening to the two men come in my door, I nearly crawled out of my skin. Even after the many warnings they'd given before entering, I wasn't prepared. I never am.

The outside world terrifies me in a way I don't think

I'll ever be able to overcome. Ryder doesn't need that in his life. He's not designed for it. It wouldn't be fair of me to lead him on and get involved. I'll only break his spirit, as well.

I want to tell him that. To say that he and Theo should leave. Go. While they can. Before my vortex of a life drags them in too deeply to back away. I should say all these things.

Except, I can't.

I haven't felt so safe as I do right now in more years than I can remember. Ryder holds this strength within his being that is unmatched to anything else.

I'm greedy and uncaring of everyone but myself right now. I want this comfort. I need it like I need my next breath. The fear of the past few days has caught up to me, and all I want is this man. I'd be lying if I said I hadn't been thinking about Ryder in his absence.

I waited by the window for the sounds of his padding feet. When they hadn't come that second day, I gave up. Not wanting to face the disappointment of another person abandoning me. I'd been sucked so deeply into my own nightmares that I haven't thought about anything else.

Sleeping and eating hadn't been a priority when I was jumping at every little sound. The wind rustling the leaves, horns honking in the distance. Doors slamming from my neighbors.

Voices…

The voices were the worst. I could never tell which ones were real or in my head. A call to my psychiatrist netted no results when I couldn't concentrate on her words. I could barely form a sentence to explain what had happened and why I was so panicked.

She was calm, rational, and reassuring. Everything I needed. Nothing I could accept. Until I heard Ryder's voice this morning, I hadn't taken a breath without panic since he left my porch that night.

I want so much to be able to live even a semi-regular life. I want to be able to go outside and feel the grass between my toes, sunbathe on my back porch. I want more than anything to have some sort of semblance of normal. Even if only for a day.

My fears have built a wall so entrenched in my mind that I don't foresee it collapsing any time soon. I know that once Ryder realizes what's wrong with me and that I've failed as a woman, he'll leave, and that's when the bricks will be cemented back in place. I'll die alone and miserable.

"Hey, you want a slice?" Ryder's husky voice is soothing in my ear. He's holding a plate with two slices in front of me as Theo hands him a water bottle.

I don't. Not really. My body usually rejects any type of sustenance when I get this stressed out. "No," I croak, only just realizing how dry my throat is.

"Come on, dove. You have to eat something," he encourages, and I see that Theo has already eaten half of a pie. "Christ, man, you could slow down and chew." Ryder laughs at him.

Shrugging, he mumbles, "It's good pie, man," and shoves another bite in his mouth.

"Code?" Ryder nudges me, but I'm too tired to sit up, let alone chew.

"I just want to close my eyes for a bit," I mumble as I feel the dark abyss float into my consciousness.

"Twenty minutes," I think he says. His voice sounds so far away, like he's talking through a tunnel.

As my body floats and my mind lets go of my fears, I briefly wonder if this is what dying feels like. It's peaceful. Sedate. There's no pain, and my emotions aren't a mess that leaves me wishing for a new life.

If this is death, I think I'll take it.

Ryder

Theo left after double checking that the sensors on the doors and windows were working and with a promise to return with Foster and supplies in the morning.

When Codie slumped over against me, real fear rushed through me for the first time in my life. A fear bone-deep and chilling because I felt everything rush out of her body like a tidal wave. I even checked for a pulse as her dead weight slid to the floor. Her fluttering heartbeat the only reason I hadn't called for an ambulance.

She is weak, there's no doubt. She needs food. But right now, I think what she needs most is to sleep knowing it's safe. That she's safe. And if I can give her that, I will.

Laying down next to Codie, I catch her blanket with my foot and pull it over us, making sure she's covered from the neck down. I wrap my free arm across her hips and hold her tight to my body, hoping she feels my presence for the rest of the night and knows nothing and no one can get to her.

I don't know what's happening between us, but I want it to continue. I want to be here for her, and her to be here for me. As strong as I am, I know I'm still fucked up in the head, and I think helping her will ultimately be beneficial for me.

Over the next couple of weeks, I have major training to do with the rest of the team, and aside from one overnight survival training trip, I'm free in the evenings to spend time with Codie. To show her that even when I'm not here, I'm with her. I won't abandon her. Whatever's happened in her past, she can overcome it, and I'll be right there with her.

Gaining her trust is going to be an issue. I know she won't give it to me on a silver platter, and I don't expect her to. I want her to learn to reach out to me when she needs it, though. It's a sure-fire way for me to show her that I am worthy of her fragile faith.

After tonight, I suspect, now more than ever, that her psyche is severely fractured. From what, I aim to find out. Tomorrow, I'm spending the day securing her house with more locks than Fort Knox, enough cameras to look like a porn house, and replacing the glass in her windows with a thicker pane.

She'll be safe again. I'll make sure of it.

"Codie?" I whisper in her ear, brushing her dark hair back from her face. "Wake up for me, dove." She doesn't move; her breathing doesn't change. If anything, she burrows deeper into my chest. "Alright, dove, for now, you'll rest. In the morning, though, you're going to let me help you."

She may not know it yet, but I'm all-in. Not only will she have me harping on her, but I know my team will support her every bit as much. If only because I'm laying claim to a girl more broken than me but calls to every fiber of my being.

I'm not sure what's going to come of us yet, but it's going to be explosive.

CHAPTER 7
Codie

y eyes pop open, startled by an unrecognizable foreign noise, and my fear corrupts the peace my mind was feeling moments ago. The warmth I felt at my back all night is gone, and I have no idea what's happening now.

Confused, I skitter back into the corner between the couch and tables and hide the best I can as I hear footsteps looming closer. Closing my eyes tight, I pray for the end to be quick. I pray whoever is here is merciful.

"Codie?" It takes a moment, but I recall the voice, and my lids open slowly as I see Ryder crouched down in front of me. Long legs covered in dark denim, bare feet, and a muscle shirt that shows, well, his many muscles. Bumps and grooves that are littered with scars and masterfully covered with dark ink.

I'm captivated by the contrast as he holds out a hand for me to take, but I can't. I need to process everything that's happening, and I do that best in a tight space.

I shake my head. "Not yet."

His boyish grin is earnest, full as he sits in front of me and waits silently, sipping what smells like a delicious cup of coffee. My eyes stray to the mug in his hand, and he naturally catches what I've latched onto as he hands it to me.

Hesitating, I shake my hands out before reaching forward to grip my favorite mug between my palms. Bringing the rich brew to my mouth, I gingerly take a sip. The perfect mix of sweet cream and coffee bathes my tongue as I close my eyes in appreciation and finally, hand it back.

With that same grin on his face, Ryder's dark blue gaze meets mine as he spins the cup in his hands and places his lips where mine were and draws a long gulp as he finishes the drink off. Stunned, I stare at him. That was a very intimate gesture. I'm not certain how to respond to it.

"Theo will be back today." I freeze. "Foster is coming with him." I'm mute with fear. New men. Strangers. Invading my home. "I'll be here the entire time. We're going to put cameras in around the house, inside and out. Replace the lower level windows with a thicker pane. They'll also be tinted so that you can see out, but no one else can see in."

I blink rapidly at the information he's giving me, and I'm not sure how to respond. "I..." I'm at a complete loss for words. I want to say no, to beg him not to let anyone in my home. "Why?" Comes out instead.

Ryder's brows draw together, and he looks at me quizzically. "So you're safe." His words are very rational, but they still don't make any sense to me.

"I don't understand."

"Trust me then. Just for today, trust that all I want to do is protect you." How I wish I could, but it's not nearly as simple as he would like to think it could be. Not for me.

"I don't..." I have to look away from his eager gaze. "I don't do trust, Ryder."

With a gentle hand, he grips my chin, turning my head back to face him. "I'll show you, Codie. I can be trusted."

A knock on the door sounds, breaking any response I would have mustered and sent me into a panic attack. My erratic heart flies through my chest, and white dots skitter into my vision as Ryder stands, a sympathetic look in his gaze, to answer the door.

He has no idea the mess he's getting himself into with me. I have to convince him it's better off to leave me alone. Maybe his friends will be able to make him listen. I'm a lost cause, and he's a warrior. I'll be a distraction that could quite possibly get him or one of his men killed.

"One, two, three." I count the disengaging locks.

Ryder

"One, two, three." Codie counts. I noticed the panic in her eyes as the knock sounded on the door. I know that when I go back in there, she's going to be in the corner hiding. Honestly, I'll be shocked if she's not hunkered down behind the sofa.

"Hey, guys." I greet Theo and Foster as they come in with the electronics that I asked them for. The windows will be delivered in a couple of hours, which will give us just enough time to get the cameras up and running and search around the premises.

"Hey, man, where's this girl that's got you all twisted up?" Foster grins ear to ear. The man is an eternal flirt, and I should have thought about that before asking for his help.

"Hiding," Theo jokes, and I shoot him a dirty look.

Mostly because he's fucking right. She is hiding. She's terrified of her own damn shadow, and I feel a bit helpless.

"Start in the kitchen, work your way in here," I bark the orders at them. I know there's not much I can do to make this comfortable for Codie, but I'll try my best to ease her into it.

"Got it, bossman." Theo salutes as he and Foster make their way to the back of the house.

"Hi, Codie!" Foster calls as he passes the den where she's hiding.

Striding back over to where I left her, I crouch down to her level and hold out a hand. "Codie," I say softly as her head lays on her knees and her body vibrates. "Let me help you upstairs." If I can convince her to get into a hot shower and some clean clothes, I think it might help her feel some control again.

Her head lifts slightly so I can see just her eyes. I'm punched in the gut with the sheer amount of terror I see in their depths.

"No one's going to hurt you." They may be loud-mouthed assholes, but they'd never hurt a vulnerable woman.

"The panic," she croaks, her throat so dry that words are hard. "It holds me hostage sometimes."

I sit in front of her, knowing this is an important confession for her. "It consumes your thoughts, right?"

She nods. "Makes you see and maybe hear things that aren't there?"

"Yes," she murmurs, tears hovering on her lids.

"Mine, too," I tell her. "My heart beats so rapidly I think it'll beat right out of my chest."

"It hurts."

"I know it does. That's why you have to get up, every day. You have to show that panic that it doesn't control you." Her eyes close, and she takes a deep breath. "You control it, dove. It's all you."

"I want to." She averts her eyes.

"Then do it."

"I'm not strong enough."

"I'll help you."

She meets my hard gaze again, and I hold out my hand, completely prepared to wait for as long as she needs to be ready when she slowly places her fingers into my palm. Gripping her delicate hand with mine, I stand and bring her with me.

Ignoring the guys in the kitchen, I walk her to the stairs, and together, we climb. Leading her into her room, I wait in the door frame as she pauses. Likely thinking of the man who broke into her sanctuary and violated her safety.

I don't say anything as she slowly begins to wander into the room and quickly grabs clothes from her dresser. Scurrying over to me, she looks to me for direction, and I nod towards the bathroom. "I'll be right out here, waiting until you're done."

The relief that swamps her face assures me of my choice to protect her. Even for something as simple as a shower. I know she's going to have to learn to rely on herself in the future, but for now, I'll help her by letting her lean on me.

Codie

I haven't had so many people in my home since I was thrown a sweet sixteen birthday party four years ago. Having someone here, experiencing my life, the waste it's become, brings forth every insecurity I've had in my entire life.

If not for Ryder…

They wouldn't be here.

I also wouldn't be trying to gain my footing.

I'm stupid for becoming so reliant on him so quickly, but he calls to me in a way I crave to understand. I thought I loved Jason all those years ago. He made my heart skip a beat, but never, not once, did he make me feel half as alive as Ryder does. Ryder pulls at me, makes me want to be better, even if I know I can't be.

After Lucas.

Lucas was my way of gaining a life, of becoming something other than a teenaged mom. He was my one good choice, and I couldn't even protect him. I failed at the one thing I started on my own, and now, I have this amazing man seeing more in me than there is.

I am a failure.

A killer.

"Oh God!" I cry into the steaming water as it cascades down my face and body. Scalding every inch it touches.

I killed my baby.

I was selfish, and he paid the ultimate price for my mistakes.

"Codie?" I hear Ryder call as he knocks on the door. He likely hears my crying.

"I'm fine," I rasp out. Even surrounded by water, my throat is dry.

Silence is my only answer, and I dread that he already knows. He has the resources to find out anything he likes about me.

"I'm coming in." His words startle me as I see the shadow of the door opening and closing. Ryder moves gingerly, just enough to brace his hands on either side of the curtain and wait. He can't see me, but I get the feeling he'd like to open the curtain. "Talk to me," he commands.

"I don't..." *know what to say.*

"Anything," he mutters, sounding out of breath. "Tell me something. Just one damn thing, Codie."

"About what?" I don't understand what he wants here.

"Your past." I freeze at his words, and when the water begins to run cold, I shiver in the spray before I see his hand sneak behind the curtain, and he shuts it off. "One thing from your past," he says as he pulls the curtain back, observing me in all my vulnerability and insecurity. Ryder sees me in my rawest form, and still, he wants me to share with him.

My head drops, shame swamps me, and I feel lifeless as I quietly confess, "I killed my son."

I don't look up.

I don't move.

I barely breathe.

Ryder remains silent. He dries my body. He helps me dress. Holds my hand as we walk out of the bathroom and down the stairs together.

Still nothing. Not a single word spoken; nevertheless, I feel his gaze on me. His very presence surrounds me. And yet, I feel as though he isn't here at all.

I ignore the background noise, the sounds of his

friends working, laughing, joking, and talking. Being free. Being all the things I wish I could be.

All I want, though, right in this very moment, is for one word from Ryder. But I get nothing. He helps me sit on the couch in the den where the window is no longer boarded up, and he walks away.

He acts as though I didn't just expose myself to him.

He leaves me.

They always leave me.

CHAPTER 8
Ryder

*C*odie dropped a bomb on me. One I wasn't prepared to intercept. In some ways, I think she did it for the shock value. But I also think it is just her. Being as blunt as can be. She's been like that from the start in an effort to push me away.

She had a son.

One she believes she killed.

I knew as soon as I opened the shower curtain that she'd had a baby. The stretch marks were a giveaway. I wasn't going to ask her about it, and I hadn't expected her to tell me about him.

Now, it's out there. She can't take it back, and I can't unhear it.

After leaving Codie in the living room, I went straight to work. I wasn't sure how to respond. If she needed sympathy or someone to vent to, I have no idea. This is as much unchartered territory for me as it is for her.

We're both so fucking broken, I wonder if we'll be worse off together than apart. Then I imagine not seeing her again, talking to her, coaxing a laugh or smile from her. Fuck, I'd kill to see her smile. Just once.

"Hey, man, what the hell is going on in that head of yours?" Foster asks, putting his tools down on the top of the ladder as we install cameras on the outside of Codie's house. I knew it was coming. I've been working silently all day, and with the sun beginning to set and Theo finishing the windows on the back porch, I knew questions would be asked.

"Is it worth it?" I ask him. He'd been married once upon a time. The woman turned out to be a complete bitch, but he was happy while he had her.

He meets my stare. Blows out a deep breath. "With the right woman, one who can be supportive and not worry you while you're gone, yeah, it's worth every damn minute."

"Codie will worry you. Every second of every fucking day." Theo interrupts, obviously hearing us.

"What are you saying?" I ask him directly. These men are my friends, my family, and I know they'll be honest, brutally so if need be, but I also know they'll support any decision I make.

"I'm saying, I don't want to go back to Syria, bro." And just like that, I have my answer from Theo and then Foster, as he nods when I look at him, too.

"Me either," I tell them honestly, and they both look relieved. "But I'm not willing to lose out on what could be everything to my life because of fear. I spent a long time in hell, and I see just a tiny piece of heaven when I'm with her."

"Then why have you been avoiding her all day?" Foster's question follows me into the rest of the evening. I have been, and that's my biggest mistake. I told her she could lean on me, that I would be here, and I've already failed on that promise.

As we put the finishing touches on the windows, make sure the cameras are up and running properly, and double check that Codie's house is secure, I walk the guys to the door after they say goodnight to Codie and close and lock the door behind them.

"One, two, three." Codie counts as each lock slides home. I smile at her voice. Some would find it annoying, I think it's amusing. It's part of her charm.

I saunter back into the den and lean against the wall and watch her as she sits on the couch in front of the window. Her fort was dismantled this afternoon, and the window was installed with only a minor panic attack that sent her running up to her spare room.

"You watch me from there, don't you?" She doesn't

answer me, but I see her slight nod in the moonlight. Walking towards her, I grasp one of her hands in mine and place it against my chest so she can feel my heart beat.

"One, two, three," she murmurs. I pull her to her feet.

Placing my hand over her heart, I count, "One, two, three."

Cupping her jaw in my hand, I slowly lower my head. A breath away from her lips, I pause, so she has time to pull back. When she doesn't, I close the distance, and her soft lips accept mine in earnest.

Sucking the lower lip in my mouth, I moan as her taste explodes on my tongue. Cherries, delicious sweet cherries. Ripe for the picking, and I want more.

Wrapping my other hand around her waist, I pull her farther into me. Feeling her small frame curve perfectly into mine, makes my dick throb, and anticipation run through my veins. I want this woman with a ferocious need I can't express.

"Ryder," she whispers into my mouth.

"Codie," I murmur back.

"You didn't say anything." I open my eyes to look at her, and even though I see a touch of need reflected back at me, I recognize her worries and fears, too.

"Because, I don't believe you did any such thing. You couldn't. The way you feel so deeply, with everything you are, there's no way you harmed your son." I never thought it for a second.

"But I failed. Miserably. And he's dead because of it." She sobs into my chest. Painful, steal your breath, suck your soul from your body, sobs, and I have to wonder just how long she's been holding this in for.

"No, dove, you didn't fail him." I'll recite those words to my dying day.

"I should have noticed sooner. I should have known something was wrong when I didn't feel him move throughout the night."

I'm piecing more of this puzzle together now. "Tell me his name?" I pose it as a question. I want her to think of him happily, to be able to remember without breaking down.

She pauses before answering me. "Lucas. His name was Lucas Ray."

"Strong name," I respond, holding her hand to my chest and pressing my forehead to hers. "Come on, it's been a long day. We both need sleep." When she tries to pull away and her body turns back to the couch, I tug her back towards the stairs. I won't force her, but I'm not going to allow her to get stuck in old habits.

———

Codie

I follow Ryder up the stairs and try not to run. Going back into my room is agonizing. It's where everything changed, where I was set back what feels like a decade in my emotional state. I hate experiencing so much terror and its control over me.

Trusting Ryder to take care of me is too easy. Giving him the reins and following along is a temporary solution to a very permanent problem. But for now, if he wants it, I'm willing to give it to him. My mind needs a break. My nerves need the rest.

He stops at the door to my room and waits for me to take the lead. Knowing without me saying a word that I need this small piece of control. The decision to enter a room that once brought me joy but now leaves me agony has to be mine.

With a fortifying breath, I force my feet forwards. My hands are balled into tight fists at my sides, and with each breath, I take a small step, and soon, I'm standing beside my bed. Exactly as I'd left it nearly a week ago.

"How did this become my life?" I murmur, momentarily forgetting Ryder is with me.

"Because hiding from our pain is easier than facing it head-on," he replies, coming up behind me and leaning his head on mine.

I see his shadow in the moonlit room as he removes his shirt behind me, then his pants. "You're staying?" I ask breathlessly as he spins me to face him.

My hands land on his chest as he answers, "I am," while his hands work my pants over my hips and slide to the ground. "In." He nods towards the bed, and I do as he says.

I'm barely on the mattress when he's climbing in behind me, grabbing me around the waist and contorting our bodies to his liking. His chest lays half on my back as our legs tangle, and one of his arms acts as a pillow for my head while the other wraps completely across my hips and holds me tight to his body.

I'm tense at first, unsure of how to do this. How to be held in a man's arms. But Ryder makes it surprisingly easy as I begin to count his breaths, and soon, I find myself drifting off to sleep. Utterly safe in the knowledge that he'll protect me. He's my shield of armor.

I'm not sure how it happens, or when, or why, but I'm startled awake, entirely alone in a bed that was occupied by two. Scared to move, barely breathing, I open my eyes, and I'm hit with a sense of déjà vu as I search my room for any signs of disturbance. Only this time, I don't have my phone to call for help. I don't have a clear line out the door and down the stairs, and I have no idea where Ryder is.

"Ryder?" I whisper, barely above a breath. Slowly turning in the bed, I scan the room as I move and watch out the door until I notice nothing amiss.

Hearing footsteps on the stairs, my heart thunders in my chest, and I squeeze my eyes shut tightly, waiting for whatever's about to happen.

A dip in the bed startles me, and I jump a clear foot in the air. I'd have fallen right off the other side if not for strong hands gripping me and pulling me forward.

"Hey, dove." Ryder's voice penetrates my foggy mind. "You're okay." His hands rub up and down my body in an effort to calm my frazzled nerves.

"I hate this," I cry softly, turning into his chest. The warmth of his body seeps into me, and my shivering begins to slow as he rocks us softly back and forth. "I'm sick and tired of being so detached I can barely function."

"We'll get you there." He rubs soothing circles up and down my spine.

"You say that like you're in it for the long haul." I try to laugh it off, but I'd like nothing more than to have someone else to share my anxieties with.

"And if I am?" My breath hitches at his words, and I gaze up at him. "What if I want to be in this for the long haul?"

I watch as his lips move, but I can barely register the words. "Why would you want to subject yourself to this life? To my life?"

He frowns at me. Saying nothing at first, Ryder guides us down onto the bed, so I'm on my back, and he's lying over top of me. I can feel his hips settle in between my thighs and flashes of skin on skin twirl through my mind as I imagine what it would be like to be intimate with him.

After the explosive kiss we shared earlier, I know it's not out of the realm of possibilities, but it also makes me want to run for the hills.

"Because I'm not an easy man to deal with, either. I'm just as messed up as you, but I have control over myself. You, dove, are a work in progress."

"But why?" I still can't comprehend the reason he would want to be with me.

"Because you make me feel alive, Codie. My heart beats stronger when I'm with you. My mind settles when I can hold you. I know what I'm getting into, and I'm more than willing to take the risk. The question is…" He pauses, and I hold my breath again. "Are you?"

CHAPTER 9
Codie

*T*he pre-dawn light crests in the sky as I sit at my kitchen table and watch out the back window. A window that is now a shade darker and makes it impossible for anyone to see inside of my home.

I don't feel the same seizing of muscles when I catch a glimpse of my neighbor letting her dog out in the morning. I don't worry she'll see me and start judging me because I never leave the house.

"Hey." Ryder comes up behind me, kissing my neck as he places a hand on my hip, and for a single moment in time, I feel normal.

I feel like we're your average couple saying good morning on a typical day.

"I have training the next couple of weeks. I'll be

gone before dawn but back in the evenings." He sits next to me and pulls my phone out of his pocket. "I programmed mine and Theo's numbers in here. If you need me for anything, you call. If I don't answer, you call Theo." I only nod. I won't call either of them, but I don't want to argue. "I mean it, dove."

"I know," I whisper, taking the phone from him.

"I'll check in around lunch, see how you're doing." That normal feeling is gone again. Carried away with any sense of comfort I was once feeling.

I'm damaged goods, and he's forced to treat me that way.

I don't want him to, but circumstances what they are, he has no choice. I'm in a hell of my own making and helpless to change any of it.

"Okay." I put my head down, silently making a list of things I can do today to keep busy and not worry about if he's going to come back. "You don't have to, you know."

"Have to what?" His voice is skeptical. Likely suspecting what I mean.

"Call me. Come back. Anything." He deserves an out.

Without saying a word, he stands, moves over to me, lifts my chin and lays a light kiss on my lips. All too quickly it's over, and he's walking to the front door. The deadbolts turn, and I count in my head. "Come lock this, and I'll talk to you at lunch."

I have no choice but to do it. Secretly, I'm elated he wants to still call me. I'm glad he's not easily scared. "One, two, three." I turn the bolts. Taking a deep breath, I try not to worry about being alone for the first time in two days, but it's hard.

Routine.

My therapist, Amy, says routine is key to breaking habits.

Until I feel secure, I'll close the curtains around the house then set a timer on my phone to open them for a few minutes at a time. Maybe I can get some work done. My inbox is filled with requests that need to be filled or customers won't get their orders.

Switching a lamp on, I carry my coffee to the computer and log in, quietly humming at my desk. It's not long before I'm immersed in my work and startled out of my concentration when my phone beeps with the timer.

Gazing at the window in the den with dread, I wonder if maybe I can just leave it for a little longer.

One step forward, three steps back. If you keep moving at this pace, Codie, you'll be trapped forever. Amy's voice plays in my mind, and I know I have to do it. I have to move past the fears and remember the glass is tinted; no one can see me.

You have to start somewhere.

Standing from my chair, I slowly take one step

forward, then another, and another, and soon, I'm in front of the window, the edge of the curtains in each hand. Pushing one back, then the other, the sun blinds me as my darkened room grows in vibrancy.

A car drives by, two women jog down the street— one with a stroller in front of her. A door slams shut, and a dog barks. Life surrounds me, and I'm stuck inside a home I once loved, trying to fight my way free.

Hunger pains hit my stomach, and I gaze at the clock on the wall to see it's nearing lunchtime already. Ignoring the itch I have to close myself off from the outside world, I walk to my kitchen, pull the chain for the blinds over the sink, and make myself some soup.

Being open like this, letting the world into my home, is nerve-wracking, but the more I busy myself, the easier it is to forget. Shadows flicker in the light, and I jump at each and every single one of them, but I refuse to close the curtains. I can't close them. I need to start taking more steps forward and less back. Which means pushing myself out of my comfort zone for as long as I can stand it.

As I'm about to sit down at my desk and work while I eat, a man slowly walks up to my house with a large box in his hands. Looking down at my calendar, I see I'm not scheduled for any deliveries until Friday—four days from now—so I pause and wait. There's a small bench on the porch in front of the window as he searches around him. He places the box down on it without trying to ring the doorbell.

Suspicions rise. I don't move as he leans forward to look inside my home. "He can't see you," I whisper to myself, completely frozen where I'm standing. Pulling away, I hold my breath as he walks over to the door. The only thing there is, is a peephole, and he certainly can't see in through there, but the door handle jiggles, and that's when I know he's not here to deliver anything.

Placing the soup bowl down, I rush to the kitchen to double check that the back door is locked and close the curtain over the sink. I knew this was a bad idea. I never should have tried to break out of my comfort zone. "Stop it," I hiss at my own critical self. I have to stay rational. I have to keep my head right and not allow the panic to overcome me.

"Think, Codie, think," I murmur as I grab a knife from the butcher block. I can still see the front door from the kitchen and the window. I'm anxious to find out what he does next, terrified to rush over to my phone and call for help, but I have to do something.

Slowly easing my way to my phone, an idea strikes. I can record him. I'm too afraid to get close to the window, but there's enough light that his shadow will be seen. Unlocking my phone, I turn the ringer to silent, knowing Ryder said he was going to call soon and click the camera's record button as the stranger comes to stand in front of the window again.

I get as close as I dare, but I can't make out his features from the shadows surrounding him as he watches me watch him. Only he shouldn't be able to see me.

"Oh god," I mumble as he tilts his head to the side, almost as though he knows I'm standing here. Maybe he does. When he turns to leave, I feel my entire body sag in relief, only to see him walk around the side of my house. "Shit."

The doors are locked. The windows are locked. Everything's tight. I have to keep reminding myself of that.

I'm safe.

The handle on the back door jiggles, and I bite my lip to keep the scream of fright at bay. This is unchartered territory for me, and I have no idea what to do. With the camera still recording, I see Ryder's name pop up on the screen as he calls.

Hitting the stop button, I answer the call with a whispered, "Hello?"

"Why are you whispering?" He's out of breath, and I can hear music pumping in the background.

"Ummm." It's not his job to worry about me.

"Codie, what's going on?" He's more alert now.

I don't know if I should tell him or not.

"Well, it's, uhh…"

"Out with it!" he demands.

"I think someone's trying to break in," I rush out, having lost track of the potential intruder. I hear a lock click on the front door. "One…" I begin to count out of habit until I realize what's actually happening. "Ryder, he's coming in."

"Upstairs, now. Spare room, in the closet, hide down low. Don't fucking hang up on me either, Codie." I do as he tells me without thought. "Theo!" I hear him yell.

Mumbling can be heard in the background, and I assume someone's answering him or asking what's wrong.

"Trip the alarm at Codie's. Someone has a fucking set of keys to her door." His voice is full of rage. "I'm coming, Codie." I barely hear him as an alarm blasts through the house, nearly making me deaf with its high-pitched sound. "Don't move from that spot!" I hear Ryder yell again.

I don't bother to answer because I know he won't hear me. My fear keeps my curiosity in check about finding out if the alarm has scared off the intruder or not. I can still hear noise on the other end of the phone. Ryder likely barking out more orders.

The longer I sit here, though, the more terrified I become. My anxiety builds up until I'm having a full-on panic attack, and I can't concentrate on calming myself down because the noise of the alarm blinds me from thought.

Dropping the phone, I slap my hands over my ears and begin counting. "One, two, three." I picture the first time I opened the door, the locks disengaging. "One, two, three." I remember the first time I saw Ryder. "One, two, three." How high they counted when I pushed a lifeless form from my body.

One, two, three seconds was all it took for my world to end.

Ryder

I'm at the facility before any of the other guys today. After a rough night with Codie, mostly, and my own demons trying to make themselves known, I was up early. Her doubts creeping in, I began to worry about the both of us. Whether either of us could ever fully recover from our traumatic pasts.

Then I wondered if we didn't have to recover so much as we simply needed to move forward. It's something a lot of people have told me in the past couple of years. I don't have to forget what happened, but I have to make peace with the person it transformed me into.

Easier said than done.

I don't know all the details of what happened to Codie's son Lucas, but I know her guilt is real. Her agony is gut-wrenching. Watching as she struggles to go about her daily life is painful. I've never met anyone so devastated as she.

"Hey, man." Weston claps me on the back as he walks in the locker room. "How'd things go yesterday? Heard she's a little rough." Fucking men, they gossip more than any woman I've ever known.

"She's..." I don't even know how to finish.

"Yeah," he mutters, like he understands. For all I know, he does. "You ready to hit the mats? Go a round or two before everyone else shows up?"

"Sure, man." After getting in the ring a few times with Hayes' man, Levi, my teammates might need a refresher. Levi has a wicked right hook that can, and has, knocked larger men than me down.

"Levi teach you anything new?" Weston and Theo bore witness to a few times the man had taken me to the mat with a grin on his face.

"How not to eat the ropes," I joke as we step onto the mat.

"Always a good thing. Rope burn sucks." Weston laughs.

Taping our hands up, it isn't long before we're dancing around each other, working out our separate frustrations as we bounce back and forth. Me taking Weston down, him sweeping my feet out beneath me. On and on it goes until we're out of breath and notice the rest of our team on the sidelines watching us with interest.

"You two have a beef or something?" Nix points between us.

We share a look before shaking our heads. "Just waiting on you guys." Weston shrugs as he hops to his feet.

"Had some time to kill," I answer laying on my back before looking at my watch. Almost ten a.m. "Shit."

"You see why I ask now?" Nix grumbles. "You two were going at it pretty hard for a couple hours. How didn't you notice?" I shrug as I stand. "Get a drink, grab your guns, we'll meet you on the range."

Theo and Foster share a look before they follow after Nix. They know my problem. I gaze over at Weston and wonder what his is.

"You okay, man?" I ask him. They've all been here for me when I've needed it most, it's the least I can do.

"Cute neighbor. All kinds of baggage," he tells me. "I should leave her alone, right?" I'm not really one who can offer any decent advice here, given the woman who's always on my mind. "I should," he reassures himself and nods like he's got it figured out already.

"Let's go shoot some shit." I grin at Wes, knowing full-well neither of us is in the right headspace to get excited about something we both love.

"Yeah, shoot some shit."

Walking into the armory, I grab my Glock and some ammo and head to the range inside. Seeing Nix, Theo, and Foster sending numbered targets out—we have to hit whatever number on the body Nix calls out—we're playing operation today. We miss our shot, and we're on weapons cleanup. Something none of us really enjoy doing.

"Theo, you're five. Foster, you're eight. Ryder, you're one, and Weston, you're four. Armed!" Nix calls. "Three, two, one, go!" Four shots ring out. Each of us hitting our marks with exact precision. "Nicely done," he commends, sounding disappointed we didn't miss.

"Come on, commander, make it easy, will ya?" Theo challenges him.

Nix smirks before answering. "Theo, armed!" He gets ready. "Eleven, three, sixteen, twenty-one. Go!" We all watch as Theo makes every shot without hesitation. None of us spend anywhere near the amount of time on the range as Theo does, so seeing him nail it isn't shocking.

"Easy." Theo grins, pleased with himself.

"Ryder, armed!" Letting out a deep breath, I wait for my command. "Five, seven, fourteen, twenty-five, thirty, go!"

Bang-hit.

Bang-hit.

Bang-hit.

Bang-hit.

Bang-hit.

"Shit," Foster murmurs as the smoke clears and the sound dies. "The kid's gotten better." I don't say anything as I remove my clip and enter another.

"Indeed," I hear Nix say. To many others, he might sound indifferent, but I hear the pride in his voice. If not for him, I wouldn't be as good as I am now. After I was healed enough to start moving around, the first thing I did was make my way onto the range. Nix was there every step of the way. "Weston, armed!" Nix calls, putting him and Foster through their paces.

We spend all morning and just past lunch on the range, conquering different patterns as Nix tests our reflexes. So far, no one is cleaning the weapons by themselves.

"Get some lunch. We'll pick up in an hour."

A phone call to Codie is all that's on my mind. When she finally answers, and I hear panic in her tone, I know something's wrong. "Trip the alarm at Codie's," I tell Theo as I start running for my truck. "Don't move from that spot!" I yell at her as Theo, Foster, and I jump in my truck. Weston and Nix follow behind.

"How the fuck does someone have keys to her house?" Foster asks, and I regret not changing them when we did her windows. "I'm calling a buddy of mine to come change those. Theo, see if you can pull up the cameras outside," he instructs while I break every speeding law posted on the way home.

I can see flashing lights as we pull up to the house, neighbors are standing outside, and three police cars are parked haphazardly in the driveway.

"Fuck," Theo mutters in the back. Barely jamming the truck in park, I hop out and run up to Codie's house. The door is wide open, the locks aren't broken, so the alarm scared the intruder off.

"Sir, you can't go in there!"

"Sir, it isn't secure!"

"Sir!"

Three cops yell as I rush past them and up the stairs to where Codie had better be fucking hiding or someone will pay dearly. "Dove?" I call softly as Theo shuts the alarm off. Entering the spare room, I see nothing amiss. The closet doors are closed, and I take a deep breath as I pull them open.

The sight before cracks my chest wide open. Codie is curled up in the corner, shaking so bad, she's cut her legs up from the knife in her hand. When I grip her wrist, she screams so loud I hear at least a dozen feet come running up the stairs.

"Codie." I sigh in relief and fear. Gently, I take the knife from her hand as she waves it around, so neither of us gets hurt. The police come barging through the door, and she screams again. "Get out!" I turn a deadly glare on the six men standing there as Theo pops his head in, alarm written all over his face as he sees the blood covering her.

"Damn, girl," he mumbles, pushing the police out of the room. Nix follows him, and sympathy enters his gaze.

"Pull her out, Tac."

Putting a hand behind her back and another under her legs, I lift Codie easily into my embrace as I carry her over to the bed. "Open your eyes, Codie," I whisper. As she does, I see they're unfocused, and her pupils are the size of saucers.

"Nervous thing like her has gotta have some Ativan around here," Nix comments and walks off.

"I'm here." I try to soothe her. "You're safe." She's nearly catatonic.

"Paramedics are on the way." Theo pops his head. "So is the district captain." Fucking great.

"Deal with them for me."

"You got it, man."

"Anything on the surveillance?"

"Yup." He grins.

"A face?"

"No." *Fuck.* "But he didn't wear gloves either." Triumph in his voice. "Weston's working on getting prints now."

"Thanks, man."

"You know we'd never leave you on your own, right?"

I look up to my best friend, the man I rely on more than any other on the bad days. "I know." I obviously don't say it enough. "She was moving forward, you know? She was fighting to get past this. Now, she's ten steps back."

"She'll get there. You'll be there for her; we'll be here to help." I nod. I never had a doubt. We're family.

But Codie? Codie has no one, and I need her to understand how much that has changed.

Codie

Darkness surrounds me. Noise deafens me. Dread fills me.

Agony assaults my body as I wait to come back from

wherever my mind has taken me this time. Protecting me from whatever harm was on its way to destroy me. I feel the menacing presence surrounding me as if it were still here.

But it can't be.

Ryder is here.

Nothing bad happens when he's around.

He protects me.

Even though he shouldn't. He should run fast and as far away from me as he possibly can before I suck him into the tornado that is my life.

He won't go though, because he's honorable. He's the type of man I wished I'd fallen in love with. Gave my heart and body to. He would have been there through hell with me.

Ryder Morrison does not need my kind of monsters.

But I can't let him go, either. He's the reason I'm finding my way free from this fog in my brain. He's the reason I see a light at the end of this terrifying tunnel. Ryder is the reason I'm going to overcome myself, my fears, my pain, these goddamned controlling demons.

Ryder Morrison is the salvation waiting for me; he's the one I want to give my heart to. And in order to do that, I have to fight free. Even when the doubts creep in and the voices are almost too loud, making me cower in their presence.

"Ryder?" I murmur. At least, I think I do.

"I'm here." His warm hand on my cheek eases the terror as I fight my way forward.

"You are, aren't you?" My voice remains low. I can sense the anger in the room, and while it worries me, it's not enough to make me recoil this time.

"Take your time, dove."

"We need to talk to you, Miss Ray!" A strange man's voice billows into the room.

"I told you to shut it," Theo snaps, making me smile a little.

"Take your time, dove," Ryder grits out again. "We've got you covered."

Opening my eyes, the room is lit only by the sun's rays, and I blink rapidly as stinging in my extremities makes itself known. "What happened?" I query as I lift my hands to see them bandaged up.

"You had a knife. The shaking made it nearly impossible to not cut yourself," Ryder explains. "Weston bandaged you up for now. Medics are on the way." I shiver at the word medics. They almost always want to take you to the hospital, and it's the very last thing I want or need.

"I'm fine." Turning my hands over and looking down at my legs, I wonder if I really am.

"It's all superficial," Ryder assures.

I'm almost afraid to ask, but I need to know. "Did you find him?"

Everyone around me freezes as I wait on the answer. Blowing out a deep breath, Ryder runs his hand along the back of his neck in clear frustration. "No. He was gone before we got here. Foster is going over the footage now."

"I recorded him on my phone." He nods. "Nothing?"

"You weren't close enough to the windows," Nix explains.

"Codie." The concern in Ryder's voice has my body tensing. "We have to move you." His eyes plead with me, beg me to accept his decision, but I can't.

"No. I can't leave." Nix glares at me from his position in the doorway. Theo shakes his head. Ryder's shoulders slump. I don't even know how to make them understand why, especially given that I don't understand myself.

"I know you've had a hard time of it, Codie, but you can't stay here. It's not safe." His voice is soothing as my world crashes around me.

"You don't get it." *I really try.* "I *can't* leave."

Staring back at his friends, Ryder says to them, "Close the door." Theo leaves, but Nix appears even angrier as he slams the wood behind him. "I do get it, dove. Agoraphobia isn't something you can control easily, but you can do it. You have to trust me to help you through."

I blink rapidly as my breathing spikes, and my head spins. Of course, he would know what I suffer from. It wouldn't have been hard to discover after meeting me the first time, I suppose. I just wish I wasn't so beaten down.

Turning my back on him, I sit on the edge of the bed and struggle my way through the emotions running rampant within my body. The fear of not being able to control outside forces is what leaves me hiding in my home.

Losing Lucas wasn't just the start of my hell. It was the catalyst. I put so much hope and pressure on him facilitating my new beginning that I didn't think about the possibility of losing him. The thought that his life would end before we began never once occurred to me, even after Jason left me. And now, as I sit here with Ryder trying to convince me to put myself out in the world, I realize I'm doing it again.

I'm relying on someone else to be my light in this dark hole I'm in. I want this man to be my everything, and that's only opening myself up to new hurts. Fierce pain would consume me faster than a wildfire if I ever lost him.

I have to let him go before either of us become more

damaged from the outcome of our inevitable tragic ending.

"I can't, Ryder." My words are quiet, but they're final, and I can feel him tense behind me, sensing something I'm not saying but comprehending deep in his soul.

CHAPTER 10
Ryder

I didn't want to leave. In fact, if Nix and Weston hadn't forced me out as Foster and Theo changed the locks on all her doors, I wouldn't have left.

I can't, Ryder.

Three simple fucking words.

Anyone would understand the meaning when hearing her tone.

I sure as hell did.

I didn't like it. Still don't. With the police around, I had to listen, though. I was forced to leave Codie when she was at her weakest and listen to Nix's speech all damn day about how she's making me lose focus. Interfering with my ability to remain objective and active on the team.

She isn't, though. If anything, she makes me want to be better. To push myself past all my limits and prove I came back more centered and stronger than ever before.

Sitting outside her house in the middle of the night, watching and waiting in the shadows for whoever is terrorizing her is the exact opposite of what I was instructed to do. But I'm doing it anyways. Someone wants her, and I have no idea why.

"You know," Theo says as he joins me across the street in the vacant house, "this is diametrically opposed to what Nix told you to do, right?" I didn't think he'd be able to stay away long. Theo knows me better than anyone else in the world. The asshole likely knew I'd be here before I even made the decision.

"Yup," I mutter as he hands me a beer and I pop the top open, taking a long drink. I wait for whatever else he has to say.

"You think she's done with you?"

I don't. "I think she's been fucking burned so bad that the prospect of sharing her pain with someone else is unbearable."

"That's deep," Theo mutters as he picks at the label of his bottle.

"She had a kid," I say, unable to imagine the heartache she went through losing him.

"No shit?" Theo's shocked.

"His name was Lucas." My heart aches for the boy I never knew.

"Where is he now? With his Dad?"

"No." I shake my head. "He was a stillbirth. She was seventeen."

"Fucking hell." My sentiments exactly. "Where the fuck is her family?" Theo is a family man through and through. He's like me; they mean everything to him.

"She hasn't told me." I wish she would have. I don't like searching through her background without her knowledge or consent, but it looks like I'm going to have to.

"And you haven't' sought them out yet?" He smirks with feigned shock.

Holding up the laptop beside me, I wave it at him. "I'm about to. I don't have a choice any longer." I've been putting it off for as long as I can. Her past might give some indication of what's going on.

"Who was the father?" Theo asks a question I intend to hunt down first.

"That's who we're looking for tonight," I answer as I pull up a search engine only our team has access to. It's more invasive than social media and harder to hack than the Pentagon.

"Where's she from?"

The black screen pops up with a single white search bar, and I type in her name, age, and a short description. "Not a fucking clue," I reply as my search goes through.

"And you're going to find out?" He laughs. "Good luck, buddy."

He forgets that this is what I do best. Uncovering information is why I'm a highly sought-after operative. It might take a while of sifting through other women with her name, but I'll find my Codie.

The wheel stops turning and up pops a few hundred hits of women with her same name and description. "How are you going to narrow that down?" Theo's skeptical question doesn't slow me down.

"Easy," I respond as I hack into the city's property records and pull up her name. Five minutes later, I have her.

"Jesus, you already had a plan, didn't you?"

"Don't I always?" I shrug.

Reading about Codie, her life in South Dakota, her parents, is incredibly sad. Her mom is a school teacher, and her dad works at the sawmill. They live just above the poverty line, and Codie is an only child. Likely because of their financial situation.

Codie always strived in school with her academics but struggled with socializing—not that shocking. She was never in trouble that I can find, and in fact, could have gone to almost any college she wanted on a scholarship.

"Whoa," Theo mumbles as he reads her bio. "What the hell happened there?" The decline in grades and attendance at school happened months before she became pregnant or I could find any social media posts about her with her ex-boyfriend.

Reading further, I see her dad was injured on the job and began drinking. He was arrested for three DUIs and one public intoxication. Her mom was even at risk of losing her job because of him.

"Fuck," I hiss when I see medical records showing months of abuse. Codie was in the hospital four times in the five months before the first photo of her and, one, Jason Jones can be found on social media.

"You think her dad was hitting her?"

"Yes." I clench my jaw.

"Jason has to be the baby's dad, right?"

After looking the kid up further, I see he's a spoiled shit who gets his way with anything. Around the time Codie fell pregnant, he and his family moved away to...

"Son of a bitch."

"You think she knows?" Theo speculates.

Jason Jones has been a resident of Summersville, West Virginia for nearly three years. If Codie weren't house stricken, I'd think she would, but the fact that she never leaves leads me to believe she has no idea.

"I don't," I say, looking up this Jason Jones guy. I don't know if this person invading Codie's life is a stalker or something else, but I do know this ex should be the first person looked at.

"College, huh? Must be nice for the kid." Yeah, must be. Codie didn't get that option. "What does your girl do for a living, man?"

"Something or other about online shopping. She filters orders and payments from some website." Glancing up, I see no new movement from her house, so I continue my search of Jones.

"And she bought this house?"

"No. Before she had Lucas, she met a decent case-worker from DCFS. Codie was homeless for a bit. The woman took her in. When she found out that she'd lost the boy, she gifted her this house. I guess the woman's father lived in it, and she never had the heart to sell. All Codie has to pay for is the land taxes."

"Lucky break."

Very lucky. She could have ended up anywhere if not for this woman.

"Feel like paying this guy a visit?" I gaze over to Theo, and even in the dark, I see anticipation in his stare. Theo loves nothing quite as much as a good fight. And if anyone has ever deserved to have someone fighting for them, it's Codie.

Codie

"One, two, three." I inhale. "Three, two, one." I exhale.

"Try without counting now, Codie." Amy, my shrink, talks soothingly through the phone while I try a few yoga poses she sent me in an email this morning.

After everything that's happened over the past week, I needed a voice of reason. Someone to understand what will be helpful to me without me having to say it. Even though I haven't a clue what it is I require.

I rarely do.

But Amy reads between the lines successfully.

"Tell me about him," she requests, and I pause. "Don't stop." She doesn't even have to be here to know I've paused in my movements.

Continuing my exercise, I talk a little about Ryder. "He's kind. Noble. Understanding. More than anyone I know."

"How does he make you feel?"

That's a loaded question. "Alive. Hopeful."

"And you sent him away?" Her tone gives away her confusion.

Stopping all movement, I place my hands on the mat in front of me and level with her. "He doesn't deserve the hell I'll bring to his life. He should be able to go out and not have to worry about me. He shouldn't have to tear his entire team away from training because I freak out."

"You had reason to freak out, though. Someone was trying to break into your home." *True.*

"I know." Lord do I ever know.

"When's the last time you opened your door because you wanted to, Codie?"

"Days," I whisper.

"How about we try now." Her suggestion comes out more like a command.

Grabbing the phone from its place beside me, I stand. "One, two, three." I count my steps as I walk to the newly locked door. Exactly three deadbolts. Just like before. Only this time, we know I'm the only one with keys.

"Start with the bottom," Amy encourages. She's talked about switching up the routine of unlocking, trying to break my habit of counting. It's been unsuccessful so far.

"One."

"Now the top."

I pause as I automatically reach for the middle. "Two." I lift my hand to the one above and turn the mechanism.

"Lastly, the middle." I know she wants to say, "without counting", but once I start, I can't stop.

Grasping the metal, the smooth feel of it between my fingers brings a sense of relief, as well as terror, when I turn the final lock. "Three," I barely breathe out.

"Now the handle." I can sense her holding her breath as I slowly reach for the doorknob. Turning it, I close my eyes and force my arms to pull the door open.

"Breathe," she whispers.

I remain frozen as my anxiety amplifies from the feel of a light breeze as it brushes across my exposed flesh. I should have changed from my shorts and sports bra into pants and a t-shirt.

"Breathe," Amy murmurs again.

"Breathe, Codie," a masculine voice commands, and my eyes pop open in shock.

"Ryder." His name comes out on a small puff of air. Standing in a pair of running shorts and no shirt, his chest glistens with sweat as he steps forward into the doorway.

"Ryder Morrison?" Amy questions.

"Yes, ma'am." His voice is husky, out of breath. His eyes are inquisitive.

"I'm Amy Stevens. Codie's therapist." I can hear them conversing, but I'm incapable of adding anything intelligent to the conversation, so I remain silent.

"She's told me about you," he responds, taking the phone from my grasp and holding it higher in the air.

"Good. I've got another client coming in a couple of

minutes. See if you can help her keep that door open for, at least, five minutes, longer if possible."

"Yes, ma'am."

"Codie?" Amy calls out. "I need to hear your voice. Tell me you're alright."

"I'm alright," I parrot.

"Good, I'll talk to you in two days."

"Bye," I mutter as the phone clicks, and Ryder sets it on the table beside us, standing just barely inside the door. I don't have time to ask him why he's here before his mouth descends on mine, and his hands are tangled in my hair.

My eyes close, my body hums to life, and for the first time since I made him leave yesterday...I breathe.

A deep, life-fulfilling breath. One that eases the pain and absorbs the beauty.

Pulling me fully into his body, I'm pressed into his chest, and I feel his heart beating out of control with mine. The flesh of our stomachs touch and I gasp from the heat exuding off of him. He takes a step back, and when I would ordinarily freeze up, he deepens the kiss. Plunders my mouth with his tongue in slow sensual slides. I focus on the feel of his grip tightening in my hair. I let loose my inhibitions and allow Ryder to take complete control of our actions.

I don't panic.

I don't fear it.

I don't worry.

I simply savor him in all his strength and glory as I try to give as good as I get.

Grasping his arms in my hands, I touch each ridge and bump. Trace his muscles and remember his power as his hands glide down my back, tickle down the backs of my thighs, and climb up under my shorts to grip my ass in his palms.

Picking me up, he turns so my back hits the door, and he presses his hard length into my core. My moan comes out louder than I intended, and Ryder begins kissing along my jaw and down my neck. Biting as he goes, leaving what I'm sure are small marks.

"Ryder," I gasp as he rocks into me.

"Stop fucking pushing me away," he growls in my ear. Shivers race up and down my spine.

"I don't want to hurt you." Finally voicing my fears is a bit liberating.

"Dove," he groans. "You can't hurt me."

"I wish that were true," I whisper as he places his forehead to mine.

"I'll show you," he vows and takes my mouth again.

My body lights up for him in anticipation, and I know things are about to change between us. I know he won't accept anything less than all of me.

Lord, help me, I want him. So much.

I ache down to my soul with this passion building

inside my body, and no one but Ryder can take it away. Relieve my desires.

"Tell me yes," he pleads in between kisses.

"Yes." I barely have the word out before he's slamming the door shut and locking it. Our lips never part as I hear each deadbolt slide home.

His taste makes me dizzy with lust, and as he walks to the stairs, I realize that I didn't count. I expect my anxiety to rear its ugly head, but all I feel is the longing to be with this man.

Ryder

I don't know what I was thinking when I came over to Codie's. I stood at her door for a good ten minutes before she opened it. Being away from her all damn night then spending hours tracking down her ex, I wasn't willing to be apart from her any longer. Even though I hadn't thought of a reason to make her believe that we are meant to explore this connection we share.

When I'd heard the locks and then saw her in workout clothes with her eyes closed, my cock grew to an uncomfortable length, and suddenly, I had my excuse. My need for her had been beating a slow drum in the background from the moment I first spoke to her.

Codie exudes pain and heartache all the while begging for happiness and pleasure.

If I can't fix one, I can damn well give her the other.

Fusing myself to her was all I could think of to get her to open her mind to the possibilities. Now, I'm about to lay her on her bed and devour every sexy inch of her frame. Her mewls of pleasure as I rock my cock against her hot core is all I need to continue my course.

Sprawled out on her bed with hair a mess from my fingers, blush creeping up her neck, and sweat covering her body, she's never looked more beautiful.

Kicking off my shoes, I drop my shorts to the ground and allow Codie a second to admire the flesh I've exposed for her. Eyes wide, mouth agape, her hands make tiny fists at her sides. I can't help but tease her. "Like what you see?"

She glances up at me quickly, and her blush deepens as she licks her lips. "A lot," is her murmured response.

Kneeling over her, I straddle one of her thighs as her legs part, and I dip my head to suck on her nipple through the fabric of her bra. "Oh!" she cries out. Brushing my hand up the length of her body, from thigh to hip and slowly up her flat stomach to her bra, I push the material up so her breasts are free.

The milky flesh begs for a good loving. Small dusky pink nipples stand straight up in anticipation. Cupping one globe, I lean back down to suck her into my mouth, nipping the surface. Her back arches, forcing me to take more of her into my mouth.

Codie's hands grip my hair in tight fists, pulling me closer to her body. Rocking my cock against her thigh, I can feel a liquidy slide making the movements smoother. Shocked, I pause when I feel the heat of her pussy against my leg, moving in tandem to my own.

"Horny little thing, aren't you?" I chuckle when she whines. Kissing down her body, I nibble on her flesh while massaging one of her tits with my hand. Her hold in my hair doesn't loosen until she feels me between her thighs.

"Ryder," she gasps as I bury my face in her cunt, inhaling deeply.

"You gonna give me some of that honey, dove?" My voice is raw with this need for her crawling up my throat.

"Yes," she cries out, "please."

Grasping the edges of her shorts, I pull the material down her legs in one smooth move. I feel her muscles tense as I spread her open for me. Dragging her to the edge of the bed, I kneel on the floor and lift her calves over my shoulders.

With a stern, "Don't move them," I gaze down at her

dewy skin and lick my lips. Salivating with the need to taste her, I slowly glide my tongue across her pussy lips. Up and down, I play with her. Not enough pressure to give her relief, but enough that she knows I'm enjoying her.

"Not fair," she groans when I caress her nub repeatedly.

"Never said I was going to play fair, dove." I grin at her growl of frustration.

Too worked up to continue playing with her, I suck the little bud in my mouth and nibble as my tongue flicks it back and forth. Her screams of pleasure fuel on my desire to give her more than she knows what to ask for.

Slipping a finger inside her tightness, I move it in and out in gentle motions as her hips rise up to my face. Pushing her back down to the bed, she digs her heel into my back, and I know she's ready for me to set her off.

Inserting another finger, I scissor them around for easier movement. Her panting, moaning, and groaning coupled with my own growing need make sending her off an even greater reward.

Freeing my fingers from her channel, I press on her clit with my thumb and start licking in and out of her hole with my tongue, slurping up all her juices as she comes apart for me.

"Ryder!" she screams into the empty room.

Not giving her a moment of reprieve, I stand up, flip her over onto her stomach and slam into her from behind. My hips thrust in rapid movement as I feel her continue to pulse around me. With hands full of her luscious ass, I close my eyes and concentrate as we're taken away into a realm of pleasure and tranquility I've never experienced before.

Running my hands along her spine, Codie shivers with the light touch and whimpers her bliss away as I thrust in and out of her in short, sharp pumps of my hips. Needing the carnality of the moment to last a little longer before I have to pull out of her sweet body.

"Fuck. This pussy. So damn sweet," I hiss between clenched teeth. I try to fight off my release for as long as I can, but when she turns her head to meet my gaze and arches her back, I can't hold on any longer.

Withdrawing free of her heat, I flip her onto her back and grip my dick in a tight fist to pump my release out on her heaving tits. "Shit," I growl as long jets of cum shoot out onto her belly and chest until I'm totally spent.

Seeing the evidence of our passion splattered on her body like paint, I trail one finger through the sticky mess before offering it up to her mouth. Unsure if she'll accept my offering, I hold my breath until her lips open wide and her tongue peeks out. Gripping my hand in her own, Codie draws the digit into her mouth before closing her eyes and moaning as she sucks up and down on my finger.

"Jesus, dove." I can't control myself as my hips mimic the way her head moves as she sucks. "Gorgeous."

Dropping down beside her, I slide an arm under her head and bring her body into my side.

"You're going to get sticky," she whispers, scandalized now that the passion-filled fog is beginning to wear off.

"Baby, I'll get messy with you anytime. Especially if it involves that pretty pussy of yours." Swatting her hand against my chest, I feel Codie relax and find that this moment might be just what we've both come to need for a long time.

CHAPTER 11

Codie

My body still aches from the loving Ryder imparted on me. It was spontaneous, voracious, incredible. Everything we both needed.

After a short nap, he was called away for training, and I immediately missed him by my side. When he's here with me, the voices hush and the doubts can't creep in. He keeps all the horrendousness at bay. When he's gone, it's easy to fall back on old habits of not being good enough.

It doesn't take much for my over-active imagination to conjure up the worst of the worst and convince me I'm nothing to him. After being away from him all afternoon, I'm still fighting off the doubts as I try to work.

Filling orders and dispatching money to companies is mundane work that doesn't take a lot of thought once you have the hang of it. I've been doing it for two years now. When the only social worker to ever be kind to me found out I was good with spreadsheets, templates, and organizing, she set me up with this job.

Debbie Johansson was a godsend I hadn't realized I'd been praying for. She not only hooked me up with the job but the house. She gifted it to me. Like it was a crockpot. She handed me the deed and the keys and dropped me off.

If it weren't for her doing that, I'm not sure what I'd have done with myself. In a lot of ways, it's absolutely a blessing, and in others, a curse. If I didn't have the house, I wouldn't be terrified of the outside world. On the other hand, if I didn't have the house, I'd probably be dead.

Losing Lucas killed me.

It was so much more than losing a child. My baby boy was everything to me, and I can't think about him without feeling the crippling pain that consumes every ounce of my being. But losing him also made me terrified to open myself up to the world again. All I saw was anguish. Death stared me in the face, and with it, he took my hope.

"Jesus, Code, get out of your head," I mumble into my hands. I hate the depression that comes with who I am now. I barely remember the girl I used to be. I don't know if she was happy or if she was as tormented as I am now.

I have to pray for a better future, though, or I'm not sure I'll be able to completely open myself to Ryder.

A knock on the door, followed by, "Codie! It's Nix Bishop, open the door," startles me into nearly falling off my chair.

Nix...

Ryder's boss?

What the heck could he want?

Slowly, I push back from my desk and stride towards the door. I almost jump out of my skin when there's another pound as I gaze through the peephole.

My heart feels ready to beat out of my chest. "Ryder isn't here," I call back, unsure whether to open the door or not. I barely know the man.

"I know. He's at the gym, but I'd like to talk to you." He looks as if he's clenching his jaw. "Please." He bites out after a moment.

"Okay," I answer, flipping the locks and counting in my head instead of out loud. It takes a very tense jaw to do it, but I manage. I inhale a deep breath before turning the knob and opening the door. Nix is...intimidating. Huge. Angry? "Come in," I say, taking a step back with just enough room for him to slip through.

"Don't bother," he instructs when I go to lock the

door again. Hesitating, my fear of this man in my home halts me from doing as my instincts force me to each time I open and then close it. "I won't be here long."

"Ummm…" I lick my dry lips and force myself to swallow. "How can I help you?"

"You need to let Ryder go," he snaps.

My gaze shoot up to him with wide-eyed surprise. "I don't understand…" I truly don't. Let him go? I'm barely holding onto myself.

"Ryder went through hell. Has the physical and emotional scars to prove it. The very last thing he needs is some damsel in distress holding him back from regaining his focus on the team." *Ouch.* He hit every insecurity I've been feeling. All the reasons I've been trying to push Ryder away.

"He seems to have a handle on things." I try hard not to look away from his rigid stare.

"He's good at faking things. He can't hide from me, though. He has to be completely honest and open about his life while a part of the team. If he's not, I can replace him easily enough." From what I've gathered after getting to know Ryder, and even Theo, he's not easily replaceable.

"You would do that? Because he's shown an interest in me?" I'm very confused about this.

"I would do that because you're a distraction he doesn't want." *Want…* It's the one word I hang on.

"He said that?" My doubts are creeping in again.

"Not in so many words." Nix looks away. "But I know him well enough to know what he does and doesn't need."

"And that's me?" My entire body slumps with sadness. Ryder's been so persistent. He's pushed past every roadblock I've thrown his way and forced himself through my door to show me he's not easily scared off.

"That's right. You're going to get him killed in the field. His head is always here with you. You're a liability we can't afford. As an important team member, we can't have that."

Something feels off. "I see."

"Good. Leave him be, and I'll make sure he leaves you alone, too." Without another word, Nix is out the door just as quick as he came, like he promised.

Emotionally, I have whiplash after that encounter.

Realistically, I have to talk to Ryder.

What we shared this morning can't be dismissed. Not with the way he loved me. The emotions I felt poured into our coupling were too strong to be thrown away so easily and without a fight.

Ryder

I hadn't meant to skip the morning of workouts planned for me. I hadn't meant to stay home and watch for any signs of movement from Codie. I hadn't meant to barge in on her and maul her into making love to me.

But it's what happened.

I finally got to show her just what she's coming to mean to me as a man. I know she has demons. Far more than I can slay on my own. Hell, I have my own monkeys on my back. But I know that if we can stick it out together, we'll both come out whole on the other side.

Holding Codie in my arms, feeling her writhing flesh against my own as we came apart was far better than I ever imagined. She was a timebomb waiting to go off, and I was lucky enough to bear witness to a small fraction of how beautiful she can be.

Running the track now with earbuds in, I allow a country mix to play through my mind, and almost every song seems to be about lovers. It's no wonder I can't get her out of my head for more than a second.

Nix was pissed when I came in late. He laced into me harder than any other time I've angered the giant of a man, but I'm not shocked. His sole focus is this team.

At nearing forty years old, all he cares about is the next mission.

When I joined the Navy, it was never with the intention of being a career man. I didn't know what I wanted to do with my life at the time, and it seemed the best option for me. When Nix came for me, I knew immediately who he was. I knew what he was going to ask before he opened his mouth, and I jumped at the chance to be part of this country's most elite team.

Task Force 779 isn't just a group of men looking for thrills. We're a team of men chosen specifically by the President of the United States. He pored over military records for weeks before selecting Theo, Weston, and I to join Nix and Foster on this newly assembled squad.

We're each the best of the best in our fields, and I'm forever grateful to be what this country needs, but I'm also a man. With a man's needs.

And Codie is precisely what I need.

Before I was captured, I might have walked away from her. I was harder then. I didn't get to appreciate life for what it was.

One big adventure.

I'm not looking for cheap thrills. Not anymore. With my shy dove, I can see an entire future laid out before us, and nothing short of death is going to keep me from achieving it.

After being so close to my own passing, I want

everything I can get out of life, and my neighbor is part of that. I know Nix is pissed and would rather I push her away. What he fails to understand at this point, is that by pushing her away, I'd be losing part of myself. It's not lust driving me to pursue her, it's my heart.

I'd watched the way Levi took care of my little sister and jealousy consumed me. I didn't think I'd find anyone I felt comfortable enough to be myself around after coming back. I never thought I'd let anyone see my scars.

With Codie, it's easy. She sees the imperfect me, and she understands all my agony.

She pushes back because she's afraid, and after everything I've learned about her past, I can't say that I blame her all that much. She's been burned in the worst way imaginable by her parents, her boyfriend, everyone. She imagined that she was going to gain someone who would love her, and instead, was brought to her knees by her own emotions.

"Ry!" I see Theo before I hear him as I come around the bend on our race track.

"What's up?" I ask as I pull the buds from my ears.

"You're not going to like it," he growls, looking pissed off himself.

"What?"

"Nix went to Codie's." *Fuck.*

"What the hell for?" Our commander would never

go out of his way to do something like that unless... "Fuck! He went to push her away, didn't he?" I shout as I run past Theo to the training center.

"Don't do anything stupid, Ryder!" I hear him call as he sprints to catch up to me.

The fucking dick. I knew he didn't want me seeing her because he thought she was a distraction and, sure, today she was. But I've proven already, in Moldova, that she will not affect my missions. If anything, she makes me hyper aware of the dangers around us.

I recognized something was up on that last operation, and that was because I wanted to go back home to her.

Slamming through the door after a thumbprint scan, I storm into the great room to see Weston and Foster scrapping on the mats. "Where's Nix!" My shout reverberates around the room as they stop and stare at me.

"Right here." The man in question comes through the hallway where the elevators lead to the parking garage.

"What the fuck were you doing?" I snap, my breathing harsh.

"Keeping you from making a huge mistake." He glares at me.

"No, commander, you were trying to keep me in line."

"Watch yourself, Tac." His snarl isn't missed by the men around us.

"Cool it, Ry," Theo mumbles from beside me.

Stepping forward, I know I'm daring the older man to a fight I likely won't win. But for this, me, for Codie, I won't back down.

"What did you say to her?"

"Nothing that didn't need saying." He turns his back on me, walking towards the weapons locker.

"Don't fucking walk away from me, Knot!" If this is the way it has to go down, I'm ready for him.

Turning around slowly, a deadly look enters his face. "You'll do good to mind yourself, Morrison. This is my team, and I'll run it the way I see fit."

"The way you see fit," I repeat. "If you want to run the *team* that way, fine. But you don't get to run our lives that way."

"She was a distraction!" he hollers.

"No, she fucking wasn't, and you know it. I knew something was off on that last op, and it's *because* of her that I was even aware of it. Thanks to her, the ambassador knows the Russians are spying on them."

"She'll get you killed."

"No, she won't. You had no right to interfere." I don't have any interest in coming to blows with a man I respect so highly, but if he doesn't back off, it might come down to that.

"You have a choice to make here, Morrison. It's the girl or the team. You don't get to have both." With that parting shot, he walks off, and I'm left angrier than when I came storming in.

"An isolated life on the team or the love of a woman?" I say it out loud so my teammates can hear what the ultimatum truly sounds like. "Easy enough for me," I say as I head for the bank of elevators.

"Whoa, wait a fucking minute here!" Theo yells, halting mine and Nix's progress. "Nix, man, you can't mean that." His own voice is filled with disbelief. I know Theo wants a family of his own one day so this won't sit well with him, either. "I mean tempers are flaring, but how can you think the love of a good woman will slow any of us down?"

My back remains facing my best friends as I see Nix turn to face the room. "A good woman?" he asks. "That's a woman that won't have you worrying when you're in the middle of a dangerous mission. That's a woman who won't have you losing your head." He looks pointedly towards me. "A good woman won't have you running in circles because she's fucked up."

I blink slowly as I process what he's not saying aloud.

Anger fuels me, and I lash out by spilling Codie's secrets. "Are you fucking kidding me? Do you know the hell she's gone through?" Nix frowns at my question.

"She gave birth to her stillborn fucking son! At seventeen, she went through the worst loss of her life, and you know what? She had fucking no one but a social worker who took pity on her. The father tossed some bills at her to get an abortion. Her own fucking parents kicked out their pregnant teenage daughter because she chose life over fucking death." I'm so livid all I can see is a red haze in my vision. "She's stronger than any man in this fucking room." Hitting the down button on the elevator panel, I stare Nix in the eye. "Including me."

I respect these men with my dying fucking breath, but not a single one of them has ever been a prisoner of war. None of them have experienced what I did in those caves. They don't know what it's like to be tortured by men who have nothing to lose.

The ding announces my ride's arrival, and I step on as Nix calls out, "Ryder, wait!" I ignore him. I've said what I need to. Now, I need to cool off. I need to find my center again.

Being here when I'm so worked up and pissed off will do no good for any of us in the long run. I know that of all the men in this building, I'm the liability because of my demons. I have to think long and hard about my position on this team if I'm going to be a functioning member of it for the foreseeable future.

Codie

Inhale. Exhale. Step.

Step. Inhale. Exhale. Step.

I'm breathing my way through walking out my back door.

Inhale. Exhale. Step.

It's not easy.

Step. Inhale. Exhale. Step.

"One, two, three." My toes touch the cool wood of my back deck, and I shiver at the new sensation. It's been so long since I've stepped foot outside. My heel drops, and the smooth surface doesn't feel as frightening as I expected. It actually feels kind of nice.

With one foot in the house and one out, I'm in limbo. I want to go farther and take another step, but I can feel the anxiety rising, and I close my eyes. I block out the sun, the trees, the soft-looking grass I want to lay on.

I don't do anything except breath.

Slowly.

Deeply.

"One, two, three." I move my foot that's inside onto the doorjamb, the metal and rubber from the insulation digging into my arch. I focus on that pain, I focus on the desire to relieve it, and the only way to do so is to step forward.

One.

I inhale.

Two.

I exhale.

Three.

I lift my foot and freeze just as I would have stepped fully onto the deck.

This is the moment. This is my do or die. Right here, right now, I can change everything. I can fail.

Or I can succeed.

An image of a smiling Ryder pops into my head, and I know I want to do it. If not for me, then for him. He deserves all my strength. To take this first step for us.

Gripping the doorframe tightly, I take a deep breath and lower my leg. With both feet now firmly planted on the deck, I continue to concentrate on my breathing and not the fact that I'm outside. I beat my anxiety down with a hammer and order my body to comply for as long as I can.

I'm not sure how long it's been, could be minutes or hours, but the feel of the sunshine on my face, the warmth that consumes me, makes my breathing come a little easier. I can see a light at the end of this treacherous tunnel, and before I know it, I'm entirely outside.

My hands aren't holding the door, my body is

screaming to turn and run back inside. I can feel...life around me. I experience a small amount of freedom at being out here.

"I'm outside," I whisper with awe. "I'm actually outside."

As I open my eyes, I gaze around my yard. Everything appears clearer. I'm not looking through windows anymore.

I'm here.

I'm in it.

This is me.

Living. Outside. Of my home.

"Codie!" I hear Ryder call from the front of the house, and I'm so excited that I can't even answer. I know the exact moment he spots me, though. The air behind me changes. It crackles with electricity as he moves closer. "Codie?" His hands glide across my shoulder, down my arms, and land on my hips where he squeezes gently.

"Ryder," I sigh. "I did it. I'm outside." Barely a step and only on the deck, but I'm doing it.

"You are." The heat of his chest against my back relaxes me further as we stand together. "We need to talk," he mumbles in my ear, and I can hear the stress in his tone.

I can already feel my anxiety worming it's way back

into my body, so I step back inside and slowly close the door, already missing the fresh air.

Turning around, I notice Ryder sitting at my small table with his head in his hands, and I can see how tense he is. All my doubts start creeping back in. My fears about not being good enough surface and begin to suffocate me.

Sitting across from him, I cross my ankles and steeple my hands on the table while I battle my insecurities internally and wait for whatever it is he has to say to me.

"I got into a fight with Nix today." *Nix.* The same man who came to see me. The one who wants me to push Ryder away.

"I see." I begin to pick a napkin apart nervously.

"I know he came to see you."

"And that angers you?"

"Yes." He stares at me. "He didn't have the right to interfere."

"Okay." I'm out of my depths with this conversation.

"I'm not in a good headspace right now, Codie." My heart clenches. "I'm going to go visit my parents and sister in Colorado in the morning." He looks at me expectantly. "I want you to come with me."

I wait for him to say something else after dropping that bombshell, but nothing is forthcoming. I have no idea how to respond. I gaze back at the door I was standing just centimeters outside of minutes ago and wonder how he expects me to travel to another state when I could barely step onto my back deck.

"I can't do that." The warmth in his eyes clouds over, and I know that's not the answer he's looking for. He wants me to say yes.

"I understand." Ryder stands, and panic consumes me at the idea that this is it for us. Maybe Nix was right after all? Maybe I am too damaged for a man like Ryder.

Damn him and his negative comments.

"When will you be back?" I follow after him like a puppy as he opens the front door, preparing to step out without saying goodbye.

He looks at me with sadness in his dark orbs, and I frown. "A couple of days." He returns my expression this time. "I'll see you soon." With that, he's gone, and I feel like my heart has just been ripped from my chest.

What just happened?

CHAPTER 12
Ryder

I was up long before the sun to catch my flight home to Loveland, Colorado. With lead in my stomach, I pulled out of Charleston. I didn't want to leave Codie. I wanted her to say she would come with me. Even if we both knew she wouldn't have been able to.

I understand that she believes she's blocked herself off from the world, but I think she's blocked herself off from…herself. Codie is so terrified of feeling pain, she's shut herself off from experiencing any type of positive emotion the world might offer.

Even after drowning in the depths of hell myself, I'm not nearly as closed down as she is, and after my blowout with Nix, I feel a void.

I'm not ready to give up on Codie, not by a long

shot, but I need perspective. I need to discover what my happiness is again, and I think my family will help me with that.

I left Theo and Weston at my place to watch over Codie in case something happens at her house again, or she needs something. I'm not entirely sure how long I'll be here for, but I feel better knowing the guys are watching her back.

After finding where her ex resides, I also learned that he's out of the country, and therefore, untouchable until he gets back. I snooped around on his parents a little bit, too, and they seem to have no reason to torment Codie. The mother is dead, and the father works and goes home as far as I can tell.

"Ryder!" Lifting my head up, I'm surprised to see Hayes standing there with Levi, her large belly leading the way. Dad was supposed to pick me up.

"Damn, girl." I grin at my sister. Even pissed at me, she's happy I came home. I've been working my ass off to gain her forgiveness, and in the past couple of months, with her hormones dominating her mind, I think we're getting there.

"Shut up." She points and glares at me while Levi holds back his laughter and shakes his head.

"What?" I shrug. "I was just going to say you look great." She's as big as a house and ready to pop any day, I'm sure. Or she's carrying triplets.

Hayes pulls me in for a hug, and as I hold the girl in my arms, I feel relief from the influx of emotions that have kept me locked down for hours. "Fuck, you look good, kid."

Stepping back, her arms fall to her sides as she says, "You look tired, Ryder. What's going on?" My sister knows me better than anyone else, and she would realize that an unscheduled visit like this is definitely out of character.

"Nothing for you to worry about, kid." I wrap an arm around her shoulder and guide her away from the terminals and over to the parkade.

"You know that won't work," Levi murmurs, so she doesn't hear as she walks ahead of us.

"No. It won't," I sigh.

"We're here if you need us, man." Levi claps my back before catching up with Hayes. I watch as he slips his arms around her waist and kisses along her neck. Hayes nearly falls, and Levi docsn't miss a beat, catching her in his arms and spinning her around to kiss her on the lips. The moment is so tender and intimate that I have to look away.

Envy burns through me because that's what I want with Codie, and I'm afraid she won't allow herself that kind of happiness.

Even after stepping outside yesterday, which I was so fucking proud of her for, I was too lost in my own thoughts that I hadn't taken the time to celebrate what an achievement that was for her. I know I'm going to have some making up to do when I get back home.

Being a broken piece in a relationship with two fragmented people is one of the hardest things I've ever tried to overcome. I know she's worth it, though. The fight, the pain, everything we're about to go through is going to be worth more than its weight in gold. I know it will.

"Mom and Dad are excited to see you." Hayes smiles up at me as Levi helps her in the front seat of their now very sensible SUV.

"What happened to the Charger?" I look at Levi, and he winces.

"Not with Hayes, man. Too dangerous," he responds.

"Oh, bite me. It has nothing to do with me and everything to do with the fact he's overprotective of this baby of ours." She glares at her man, and I have to laugh.

"Can't say I blame him." If I ever get the chance, I'll be the exact same way.

"We're going to drop you off at your parents, and then Hayes has an OB appointment. We'll be back for dinner, tonight." The hour's drive to my folks is quiet even though Hayes asks me a million questions about what's been happening.

After everything that's transpired, my family still

doesn't know exactly what it is that I do. They know I'm on a special forces team, but they don't know about the dangerous missions. They don't know that on any task I could be arrested, and the US government would abandon my squad and me. I hate having to keep secrets from them, but it's part of my contract.

The president may be in charge of us, give the orders, but if we're ever caught, he'll deny our existence. I'd always been okay with that. Until I was captured. Until I acknowledged that I was a lost soldier.

I didn't doubt that my team would come looking for me. Even after they found a burned body in a cave with my tags, I knew they wouldn't stop until they knew the truth. After a year of waiting, when they *did* rescue me, it was my choice to leave my family in the dark for so much longer. I hadn't wanted to come home less than whole.

Whatever that means.

"Here you go." Hayes smiles back at me. "I'm glad you're home, Ryder."

I lean forward and place a kiss on her forehead. "Me too, kid. Me too." Stepping out of the car, I stand on the sidewalk for a few minutes before walking up to the house in search of some semblance of peace.

"Ryder!" I'm not even halfway up the walkway and Mom comes running out of the house. "Oh honey, I'm so glad you're here!"

Catching her in my arms, I drop my bag and lift her up for a big hug. "Hi, Ma."

"Son," Dad greets from the door. "You look tired." Could he be more like Hayes?

"I am," I reply honestly. I won't worry my sister, but this is why I came home. I need clarity from people who understand me better than most. I carry demons that have to be conquered before I can go back to the team.

"Come in, come in." Mom ushers me inside after she grabs my bag. "Your room is all ready for you. Dad has some coffee in the kitchen with those muffins you like. I'll be right down."

Even when my family thought I was dead, they didn't really lose hope. After I came back, I discovered that they had a room set up for me. Like I'd gone on vacation and not been killed in action.

My parents are the most faithful kind of believers, and right now, they're exactly what I find myself needing.

"Well, what brings you home?" Dad and I have always been close. He can read me like a book. It's no surprise he knows there's something going on.

"A girl." He grins, and I can't help my own smile. "She's even more screwed up than me." I don't like talking about my time in captivity any more than they like hearing about it, but it's part of who I am.

"Tell me about her." He hands me a black coffee, and I stare into the circling dark liquid. The shade matches my mood.

Codie

Mornings are meant to be the dawn of a new day. They should signify a fresh start. Mine is anything but. I haven't slept since Ryder left. I stayed up analyzing everything he said to me.

All that Nix accused me of.

I stayed up all night going through the pros and cons of a relationship with Ryder, disregarding his commander's feelings towards us.

There are plenty of pros. More than I could have thought possible.

And only one con.

Me.

I'm the flaw in our relationship.

The broken piece.

I'm where our love will come to die.

After staring all through the night at the piece of paper with the single word on it, I've come to a conclusion. I want this with Ryder. I've gone through so many scenarios in my head about how my life would be without him in it, and all I see is darkness.

Ryder signifies hope.

My hope.

He's my chance at starting anew. He's my new beginning.

With a renewed sense of determination, I search through the footage from the cameras recording around the outside of my house and find that whoever has been trying to scare me hasn't been around for a couple of days. With that in mind, I'm determined to make today the first day of the rest of my life.

With slow steps, I plan to become more open to the outside world. My first mission is finding out how the sensors on the screens of the windows work.

Ryder gave me Theo's number, and I get the feeling that if anyone on their team is going to help me, it'll be him. So, I send a short message.

Me: It's Codie. The sensors on the screens, what do they do?

I'm not familiar with how alarm systems work and most especially not this high tech of one. It doesn't take him long to send a message back.

Theo: I'll be right over.

That's not quite what I anticipated, but I'll take it. Wanting to make the first move as this new, determined me, I walk to the front door and undo the locks. I open it just as Theo is about to knock.

"Shit. Sorry." He laughs as his fist comes inches from my nose.

"It's okay. Would you like coffee?" I should be friendly with Ryder's friends, right? I've never done this before. Maybe I should look up online how to be a proper partner.

"I'm good. I was on my way to the gym." He nods. "What do you want to know about the screens?" His attitude towards me feels cold, and I suddenly regret asking for his help.

"Umm, if one of them pops out, will an alarm go off or something?" My hands won't stop fidgeting under his scrutinizing stare.

Theo stares around the room before finally answering me. "The alarm won't blare, but the panel"— he points to it on the wall behind the door—"will beep consistently until you turn it off. Same with your phone, and mine, until it's shut off." I catch how he doesn't say Ryder's name, and my heart squeezes tightly. "However, if it's not deactivated in a certain amount of time, then an alert will go to the police department."

"Alright." That's more or less what I wanted to hear.

"Why?" His gaze narrows on me.

I don't know Theo well enough to be completely

honest with him, but I do trust that he's an honorable man. "You know that Nix was here." It's not a question. I get the feeling they all know what each other is frequently doing. "Actually, he made a few valid points."

Theo nods, not disagreeing with me. "Go on."

"Well, Ryder appeared unimpressed with my progress yesterday." That still hurts like hell. "And I guess, when he comes back, I want him to want to come see me again." I blow out a deep breath because admitting it out loud—how I failed another person—isn't easy. Especially when they're coming to mean so much to me.

"Progress? What progress?" His head tilts in confusion.

I almost smile until I remember how ignored I was. "I stepped outside the back door. Ryder came in while I was there, and I suppose it wasn't enough." I try to shrug off the hurt and look away from him.

"Are you fucking kidding me?" An enthusiastic smile erupts on his face, and a weight lifts off my shoulder. "Codie, that's fantastic!" This was what I anticipated from Ryder.

"Thanks." I turn my head sheepishly.

"Don't take his reaction to heart. He and Nix really got into it. Worse than they ever have. Ry needs some time to clear the cobwebs, but he'll be back." Theo places a finger under my chin and lifts my head, so I have to meet his stare. "Don't think for a second that what you did was anything less than amazing." I nod. "Good. Now be careful, be aware, and call if anything happens. Try to keep things locked up on opposite sides of the house you're not in."

"I will. Thanks, Theo." This time he nods before jogging down the steps and to his bike parked on the street.

Shutting the door behind me, I gaze around my house with plans in mind to transform my life and give myself a mini fresh start as I begin opening windows to let the breeze filter through.

CHAPTER 13
Ryder

"Are you sure you'll be alright, Ry?" Hayes' mothering skills have been put to the test the last two days, and she's taken every opportunity to push her way into my business. After spending some time with Levi and his brothers at their mechanic shop, and seeing the easy comradery they have with each other, I can't say I mind much. Hayes and I were that close once, and after this visit, I feel like we're almost there again.

"Yeah, kid, I will be." Being home has done wonders for me. My head is clear, and I feel like I've seen the light. Dad has always been my sounding board, and after a long talk with him, while Mom hovered, I was able to gain a bit of perspective. He helped me to understand Nix's worries about the potential of Codie being a distraction. And while I don't agree with his methods, the text updates I've been getting from Theo certainly seem to prove that maybe Nix was right.

"You make sure you apologize to her." My sister points her finger at me with a scowl. We stayed up late last night talking about Codie, and I shared some of her story with Hayes. After she drug out how I left things, my sister was pissed. More so than when I came home.

"I will." She has no idea how much I will.

"And you'll video call me soon, so I can meet her." It's not a question.

"As soon as she's ready."

"And you'll find her parents?" That more than anything else angered the little spitfire. She was ready to go knocking on doors and kicking asses—or rather, sending Levi in to do it. Thankfully, my brother-in-law had seen the direction his girl was going and sent her to bed.

"After I apologize."

"And grovel. You can't forget to grovel. Because she deserves that." Tears well in Hayes' eyes again, and I pull her in for a hug as my flight is called to board.

"I'll grovel," I promise, kissing her forehead as Levi holds her back and gives a wave.

"Call me when you get home!" Hayes yells as I hand security my ticket. "After you grovel!" I shake my head at her and gesture goodbye as I'm waved through the line.

Lord love the girl, but she has no filter. Lucky for her, that's one reason Levi loves her so damn much. Never thought I'd see someone so big and intimidating as him fall for such a hellion like that sister of mine. But their love is what movies are made of. Never could anyone miss the way they adore each other. Until I saw them, really studied them as a couple, I didn't believe in soulmates or true love. They were an enigma to me.

I know my parents love each other deeply, but I'd never seen them look at each other the way Levi, and even his brothers, look at their girls. But coming home this time, I recognized how much love Dad has for Mom.

It was undeniable.

I wasn't a believer before. But I sure am now. And I believe that the feelings that are unfolding inside me for Codie are going to become exactly what I've been witnessing for days.

Now to get home and do that groveling Hayes says I have to do.

Codie

I've spent the last day and a half working on creating a better flow in my house. Making it work for me, rather than me working to hide from the world. I moved my desk in front of the big window in the living room/den so that even when I'm glued to the screen for hours on end, I can still see the wonder of nature and life surrounding me. I got rid of the blackout curtains and enlisted Theo and Weston's help to pick up new ones I ordered online from Target. They grumbled at first but relented when I promised food.

We've gotten to know each other a little better over the last couple of days, and though they're Ryder's friends and teammates, I feel as though I can call them friends now, too. Even after I insisted they didn't have to help move some of the heavier furniture. They persisted and worked on it after finishing their training during the days.

Ryder hasn't contacted me since he left, and while I can sometimes feel myself falling into a sinking hole of depression, I remind myself of what Theo keeps claiming.

He needs time.

If anyone can understand that, it's me. Time is either your enemy or your friend. In this case, I'm hoping friend.

Gazing out the window, I can see storm clouds rolling in, and I hope I'm able to continue with my exercises before the rain dumps down on the city for what the weatherman is predicting to be the largest rainfall of the year.

Every hour, I've been stepping outside for just a few minutes at a time. Getting my body used to feeling what the world is like before the anxiety takes over and I'm crippled with fear.

Today, I plan to try for an extra step forward on the front porch. A neighbor looked at me like I'd lost my mind last night when she was walking her dog and saw me. In all honesty, it was probably the first time we'd ever made eye contact.

I smiled as she passed and even gave a little wave. She frowned and hurried her dog along. I forced back the feelings of inadequacy and doubt and stayed out for a few more minutes, trying to keep the faith I had flowing through me.

Opening the front door now, the breeze feels cool. The scent of rain is in the air, and I get the urge to dance in it like when I was younger. Sitting on the doorjamb, I spread my legs and feet out in front of me instead. Accepting that I can do this and handle the emotions and memories as they bombard me.

"Mommy, watch me!" I was five when I discovered how much fun running through puddles could be. "I love my

boots!" I can hear little me screaming from the driveway as my mom gazed upon me in the middle of a stormy afternoon.

Those boots were the best part of my young life. They meant I could run and play, splash as much as I wanted to, and Daddy wouldn't get mad at me for ruining my tennis shoes.

"Quickly, Code, or you'll catch a cold." Mom smiled so much when I played in the rain. She would laugh and cheer me on from our front door as I kicked up the water and squealed when it splashed me back.

"But I wanna live in the rain!" I remember wishing for a Paddington Bear every day after that. The one with the rainhat and jacket. I prayed with all my might for that bear. When Christmas finally came, and he was sitting under the tree, I grabbed my coat and boots, and lucky for us it was a warmer winter, so we had more slush than frozen snow. For hours, we played outside, discovering the world around us.

I was free to be a child. Being loved by parents who would later abandon me wasn't a worry on my mind. Losing a child of my own hadn't occur to me.

I feel a tear slip free as I remember when life was good. I don't brush them away, I embrace them. I accept my loss, and I know it's time for me to heal.

For early afternoon, the neighborhood is quiet, and I enjoy the solitude the work week provides as I begin to spread my wings. Learning to fly on my own is not nearly as harsh as learning to breathe again after Lucas.

I haven't been home to visit his grave since the day I buried him. I cried and cursed so much that day, and all the ones before and after, that it's blurred together. It seems silly, but I don't have a single untainted memory of Lucas. Even pregnant, I was filled with resentment, harbored so much anger for everyone that left me to fight my way through the scariest months of my life.

My parents for kicking me out.

Jason for calling me a whore.

His parents for throwing money at me like I was a problem to be solved.

Myself for being weak. For abandoning my hopes and dreams because of such a tragic loss.

Forgive to heal.

Amy says it to me every time I call her in a panic. The forgiveness isn't for those who did me wrong, but for me. So I can move forward. I have to let go of the bleakness in order to embrace the lightness.

Much easier said than done.

It's not that I don't want to. It's that I'm afraid once I do, I won't have anything left to fight for. I'm terrified that if I move past the anger, hopelessness will take over and I won't escape.

One, two, three. I hear his steps.

Lightning blinks across the sky as I look up to see Ryder jogging past my house.

One, two, three. He's past the hedges.

I hold my breath, wondering if he saw me. If he missed me as much as I missed him.

One, two, three. He's back.

I climb to my feet. Even from the street, I can see the huge grin across his face as he notices me outside of my comfort zone.

Ryder takes a step forward.

My feet move.

He takes another.

I do, too.

He runs forward, and I find myself on the top step of my porch, unable to go further but elated as he comes to me. Seeing him opens a crack in my heart, beats down the walls I've been erecting for years.

"Ryder," I sigh into his neck as he picks me up and holds me tight.

"I'm supposed to grovel," he mumbles in my hair.

"You are?" I say. Uncaring that I'm no longer covered by the porch overhang.

"Yeah. Hayes was insistent. Whatever you want, it's yours. Anything. The sun, the moon, stars. Ask for it, and I'll make it happen." With the serious tone to his voice, I have no doubt he'd do everything in his power to make it a reality.

"You. I just want you, Ryder." There's nothing more in the world I want than him.

Dropping me to the ground, I feel grass between my

toes, and before I have a moment to panic, his lips are on mine in a deep kiss that I feel down to my feet. His hands span across my back, dragging me in as close to his body as I can get, and I savor it.

This is *the* moment.

The one everyone craves. The one where they know beyond anything else that they've done it. They've found the other half of their soul.

This moment is ours.

As our kiss breaks apart, the sky opens the flood gates, and I feel it...

Rain.

For the first time in two years...I feel life. I feel cleansed. Forgiveness. Hope and healing.

"I missed you, dove," Ryder murmurs into my ear as I try to hold him a little bit closer.

"I missed you, too," I whisper back as my toes flex around the blades of grass. It's been so long since I've felt anything but carpet, linoleum, or hard wood under my feet that I'm overwhelmed, and I begin to cry. My body shakes, and Ryder gazes at me with worry in his eyes.

"Let's get you inside." He picks me up, and I want to protest but all the emotions are colliding, and one stands out among the rest...

Panic.

"My meds," I hiss out as he steps through the door. I

know this is going to be a doozy of an attack as he places me on the couch that is now against the bare wall where my desk used to be.

His hands leave me as he goes in search of what I need; meanwhile, I'm held captive in the dark recesses of my mind as I'm brought back to the day where I started to spiral out of control. Where my life felt like it was coming to an end.

"Codie," my mother cries brokenly. "How could you be so foolish?" My father stares at me like I've crashed through the house with my car.

"I'm sorry," I mumble, full of remorse and sadness.

"Sorry doesn't fix the problem," Dad snaps with a scary look in his eye. "Where's Jason? Why isn't he here telling us with you?"

My lungs seize as I try to get the words out. "Jason," I croak out and have to clear my throat. "wants nothing to do with me now." I look away from them as I say it. Jason had been so angry with me. Like it was my fault both birth control pill and a condom failed us.

"Can you blame him?" my father barks, and Mom now wails. A blade pierces my heart. "You've ruined his life." Ruined? *"He had his entire future ahead of him. Now you've gone and fucked up for the both of you."*

"I didn't mean for this to happen." I try to reason with the man I've only ever wanted to love me.

"You'll have an abortion." He levels me with a glare. "Your

mother will take you in the morning." He says it like it's final. Like I have no choice.

Wiping the tears from my eyes, I take a stand. "I won't." I've kept the secret of a life growing inside of me for three weeks now, and I've come to love him or her like they're already here, and I won't discard them like waste. I can't.

"Excuse me?" He turns a lethal glare my way, and I nearly cower. But I know I have to remain resolute or I won't be able to hold my ground. "Young lady, you are seventeen and still under my roof. You will do this, or you're out."

"Clark!" Mom finally speaks up. "Codie can't do this on her own." She comes and grips my hand in hers, wanting to help me but torn between the two people she loves most. I've never doubted her love for me, only my father's, and today proves what I've always thought.

He doesn't care about me.

"I won't have a whore living under my roof. She has the abortion, or she leaves." He crosses his arms and lifts his chin, the snarl of a snake on his mouth as he challenges me.

Gazing at my mom, I know what I have to do, even if it hurts. "I love you," I whisper.

"No," she whines. "You stay. Clark, she can't leave. She's our baby!" My father has made up his mind and won't be swayed.

"It's okay, Mom. I'll be okay." I kiss her cheek, grab the bag from beside the stairs I suspected I was going to need, and walk out the door of the only home I've ever known.

The wood slams.
Locks click.
One, two, three.
Thunder claps.

Ryder

"Min 'anat?" The masked man asks in Arabic again as another kicks my legs out from under me. I only shake my head. I couldn't speak even if I wanted to. My lips are so swollen, I can barely feel them.

"Tahadath 'aw 'amut amrykyh." Another man snaps. I'm already dead, so what's the point?

"Go fuck your mama," I spit out.

Dropping my body to the ground, all four men begin kicking me. Trying to cover my head with my arms, I feel when a rib cracks. When my wrist breaks. A gash in my skull.

All the pain, the agony, writhing through me right now is nothing compared to what I know is coming. My team thinks I'm dead. My country will have no record of me. My family has likely already grieved for me.

Maybe mouthing off wasn't the best idea, but I won't die without a fight. And a fight is what they're in for with me.

"Ryder?" A soft voice breaks through the violence surrounding me. "Ryder, wake up." Soft hands brush my face. This isn't right, she shouldn't be here.

Startled, I blink rapidly as the fog of my past falls away as quickly as it came. Codie sits above me, a look of worry upon her face. While her eyes are haunted from whatever overcame her, I hadn't even noticed when she passed out.

"What time is it?"

"Nearly two in the morning," she whispers.

Jesus. After I was able to penetrate the cloud of her own nightmares and get her to take the Ativan, I passed out not long after. Maybe mid-afternoon.

"Shit." I scrub a hand down my face as I sit up from my position on the floor in front of the couch where I'd lain her down.

"Are you alright?" Her tentative question has me looking up to her.

"I didn't hurt you, did I?" I haven't had the nightmares nearly as often in the past few months as I did the past, but when I do, they can be long-winded and violent. I've never had one with anyone around except Theo or Weston.

"No." She shakes her head. "But you were moaning,

and it sounded like you were in pain." I was. Then. As it happened. But it got so much worse after that day.

"Is it still storming outside?" I need to change the subject.

"Raining. But the thunder and lightning ended about an hour ago." Codie still eyes me critically. "Theo texted me, too."

Climbing onto the couch, I lean back and pull Codie into my arms. Settling us both before asking, "What'd he want?"

"Just to check in." She pauses, and I look down at her even though exhaustion is pulling heavily on me. "With me."

"Good." My heavy eyelids close as Codie cuddles into my chest. Contentment rolls through us both as the exhaustion of the last few turbulent days catches up to us.

We have a lot to talk about, but there's nothing that can't wait until morning. I'll be here, and I'm not going anywhere. Not ever again.

CHAPTER 14
Codie

*O*ne, two, three. I think it's him I'm counting for. His heart as it beats, his chest as it rises. *One, two, three.* As it falls. Ryder came back, and he came to me. A miracle as far as I'm concerned. Theo tried to keep my hopes up, but I remained skeptical.

I've always known there was something wrong with me. Even before my life fell apart, I felt a shifting in the air when I would walk into a room. I'd get looks of censure for no reason other than breathing. I hated it. I was confused for so long.

When I fell pregnant with Lucas and nothing had changed, and the shock you expected didn't take root, I broke a little inside. It's like everyone knew my life was over before I did. They knew I was a mess.

One, two, three.

I can't stop the counting. Over the past few days, I've come to realize it's more than just a quirk or habit. It's what I need to continue on with my life.

If I'm going to beat this phobia, I need a coping mechanism. Counting is it. I can do almost anything as long as I count.

"I can feel your lips moving," Ryder murmurs as his head lowers, and I sense more than hear him inhale as he breaths in and out against my head.

"Do you think I can get through this? Past my fears?" Right now, my biggest worry is that he'll tire of waiting for me to gain control again.

Lifting my chin with a gentle hand, Ryder's eyes soften as he searches mine. His strong jaw relaxes from its ordinarily tense stance. "You already are," he whispers. His head lowers, and I raise up to meet him.

Being with Ryder is the only thing in my world that makes sense anymore. He helps me forget my past. The anguish that tries to overthrow my every move slithers away like fog in warm air. I feel whole with him.

Ringing in the background forces us to pull apart as Ryder curses, and I lick my lips. Savoring the taste of him as he scowls at his phone. "You have to go," I say. It's not a question.

"We've been called for a rescue mission," he replies, cursing under his breath. "I can stay." He gazes at me.

I see so much in his stare. He wants to stay, but his

loyalty to his team, to this country, means he must go. I won't stop him. This is obviously his calling. What he's meant to do.

"You have to do it, Ryder." Placing my hand on his jaw, I rub my thumb back and forth, and he closes his eyes before turning his face to kiss my palm.

"You'll be here when I get back?" He frowns as though I would actually leave.

"I'm not going anywhere."

"I'll give you my sister's number. You call her whenever you need to." I probably won't. I'm not that bold. "Better yet, I'm going to give your number to her and my mom. They'll be in touch with you." He smirks at my shocked expression, knowing me well enough that I wouldn't contact his sister.

Standing with him, I follow Ryder to the door, and before he steps outside after unlocking it, I kiss him. Deeply. Touching his soul with everything I feel in the hopes he understands what I'm unable to say with words.

"I'll be back, dove."

"Stay safe."

"Always." He kisses me lightly again, just a feather touch, and he's off and gone on his next mission. I don't know how long I stand in my doorway for, but when storm clouds come crashing through the morning light, I close and lock it.

"One, two, three." My anxiety is growing as turbulent as the angry thunder crashing through the skies. Menace is in the air, and I'm not sure if it's my imagination or not, but I know something bad is going to happen.

Ryder

Leaving Codie so soon after I just got back wasn't in the plans, but a woman has been kidnapped by a drug cartel in Mexico, and she needs help. Her father runs the CIA, and because of that, the bureau won't send anyone in to rescue her. A conflict of interest, they say.

"What's it looking like?" I blurt out as I rush off the elevator to see everyone standing around talking.

"Glad you could make it." Nix nods at me. It's all I'm going to get in so far as he's glad I decided not to quit. "Everett Gaines has been taken from her vacation villa by the Diablos Cartel. They're the worst in the country according to her father, who has had a team watching and infiltrating them for years."

"Why'd he let her go there then?" Weston barks out what we're all immediately thinking.

"They're estranged," Nix explains.

Walking in front of the computer system that I'd spent months setting up to work every angle I could before we go on a mission, I jump onto our secure server and do a quick search about the girl.

"Everett Leslie Gaines, twenty-two years old. Born, raised, and lives in Phoenix, Arizona. Accounting graduate from the University of Phoenix three months ago. Mother is living in Phoenix as well, works at a law firm as a legal assistant. Nothing looks out of place." I scroll a little more, but nothing catches my attention. "If this is for money, they'll want a ransom. We should be looking into her father. Is he saying anything?"

Nix scowls before shaking his head. "Director Gaines insists it can't be about him because he has nothing to do with the day to day operations. He signs paperwork and approves assignments. Nobody but the CIA would know how he's connected to any missions."

"Coincidence?" Foster asks with a raised brow. It's not entirely out of the question, but none of us will believe that.

"Not likely." Theo speaks my thoughts.

"We're wheels up in one hour. Get your gear squared away, pack light. We're not sanctioned in this country, so you know the drill. If they catch us, we're on our own." Nix gives a nod as he walks back to his office.

"We're jumping?" Foster grins. Not much he loves more than an adrenaline rush.

"Looks like," I respond as I continue to dig into the background of the Gaines family. Everett hasn't put her degree to use yet, so it's unlikely she's involved with money laundering or anything else the cartel could target her for.

The mother works for a law office that mostly deals with mortgages and rental properties, so unless she stumbled upon a stash house in the U.S. that the cartel uses, I just don't see her being the problem.

Which leaves the director.

Bureaucrats never leave a good taste in my mouth, so I intend to search more thoroughly into his background before I can firmly say he's beyond suspicion.

It's entirely possible this is a coincidence, but for the sake of the girl, I refuse to leave any stone unturned.

CHAPTER 15
Ryder

$\mathcal{I}$ knew we shouldn't have fucking come. From the minute our plane was in the air, everything felt off. The information we were given. The lies we were being told.

The only truth we've found since landing is that the girl had been captured. Bloody, beaten, tortured, and raped. She's a fucking mess.

"I'm going to kill that son of a bitch," Foster growls through clenched teeth. I've never seen my friend so pissed before. The way he watches the girl, passed out from pain and likely blood loss, leaves me to wonder if he's just angry about us being caught and what they've done to her, or if there's something more.

"Not before I do." I hold my dirty shirt against the

bullet hole in my shoulder. All things considered, it could have gone worse. Nix, Theo, and Weston were able to get out. Shit hit the fan before we could fucking react.

We had the girl. We had an exit. We *have* a motherfucking mole. And it comes straight from the CIA.

24 HOURS AGO

"Go, go, go!" Jumping from the back of a plane never gets old. There's one second of absolute fear before freedom rushes through the blood. We fall at thirty thousand feet into a jungle filled with trees below. Into the middle of nowhere. A plan already in place.

I was able to find out where the cartel is holding Everett, and it appears to have minimum security around her. We should be in and out in twenty-four hours or less. She'll be home in the arms of her mother in two days tops.

We're jumping right in on this one. We all know the faster we're in and out the better. Mexico is not somewhere anyone wants to be captured or arrested. And since we're at risk for both, we know not to take our time on this mission.

"Comms check?" I whisper through the secure line.

"Chaos. Check."

"Knot. Check."

"Phantom. Check."

"Shaker. Check."

"Let's do this," I command.

Phantom and Knot are creating a distraction throughout the front of the compound with an explosive Chaos handed off to them, while he and I get the girl from the building in the back. Only three guards surround her, and we know we can extract her from them. Shaker is waiting with medical supplies a mile away.

"Set to blow in, three...two...one." A loud boom breaks the night air, and Chaos and I move forward through the tree branches slapping us in the face. Past the rushing guards as they race to find out what's happening at the front of the compound.

"Dammit, Chaos," Nix curses.

I look back at my friend to see him with a huge grin on his face. "He's going to beat your ass one of these days," I comment as we reach the wall we have to scale.

Tossing our rope and anchors up and over, we begin to climb. Hand over hand, up we go. Gazing briefly on the other side to make sure the coast is clear, we grab the ropes and drop to the ground silently.

"Which building?" Chaos asks as gunfire explodes from the front of the buildings.

Staring at the screen on my arm, I watch for unmoving

heat signatures, and when I see the one I'm looking for, I point to it. "That one."

Rushing to the structure, Chaos has a knife up and through one guard's chin before the man knows we're here. Blood rushes down his neck to stain his shirt. Circling to the front of the building, I've got my arms around the neck of another and squeeze until he stops flapping around. After hiding the bodies from immediate sight, we work on getting inside.

"Hurry up," I hiss as Chaos fights to free the lock on the door, and I watch for the third guard that's supposed to be here.

"Got it." The door opens and we rush in, closing it behind us just as voices can be heard. "I'll strap her on." Neither of us can see or hear Everett, but I know she's in here. "Fuck," Chaos mutters. I assume he's found her.

"Times ticking." I can now hear three distinct voices.

"This isn't fucking pretty, man," Chaos groans as we hear her weak voice.

"Please don't hurt me again." Agony exudes from the quiet words, and I can't help but feel for her.

"Ready," Chaos says.

Lifting my M249 automatic, I exit gun first, finger on the trigger and prepared for battle. Another explosive lights the night up, and I'm able to see for a split second that the open space to the wall is clear.

"Sixty seconds," I mutter as we start running, Chaos and

the girl ahead of me. *Covering their backs, I wait for him to start climbing before slinging the weapon across my back and start a hand over hand rush to the top.*

"Over there, on the wall!" is yelled just as I reach the landing. A shot is fired, and my shoulder takes the hit, falling to the ground as Foster hits with his feet. I'm winded.

"Fucking run," I bark out at him.

"I won't leave you again." He grips my arm and pulls me to my feet. Blood loss is quick, and the more I run, the more adrenaline pumps through me.

"Knot, get him out of here," I hiss.

"Keep going! We're on our way to you!" Knot yells through the line.

Every mission is always a risk. I knew this could be the end. I just didn't think it'd be over so quickly. "We aren't going to make it," I mumble as another bullet rips through my thigh, and cartel men surround us. "You should have fucking left," I snap at Chaos as he tries valiantly to keep the girl close to him.

Dropping to the ground, I raise my hands. Already knowing these men will likely kill us before they take us back.

Should have listened to my gut.

This mission was fucked before we were ever in the air.

PRESENT DAY

"Sshhh, girl," Foster murmurs to Everett. We've been trapped in this hell for almost thirty-six hours now, and she's getting worse. When we grabbed Everett, she was nude and cut to shit. We knew getting her out was risky.

Since then, Foster has given her his shirt and shared every ounce of heat he can with her, but infection is setting in, and she's sick as a dog. If we don't get out soon, I'm not certain she'll make it.

"How you doing, man?" Foster nods to my shoulder and thigh. Shoulder hurts like hell, but the bullet was a through and through. The thigh was a graze. Nothing I can't handle.

"Codie's gonna be pissed at me," I say, unable to think of what her reaction is going to be.

"I don't envy you." He laughs. Ev whimpers. "We gotta find a way out." His whispered words echo my thoughts exactly.

"They won't leave without us." Not a single member of our team is the kind to leave a man behind.

Foster levels me with a look. "We were forced to last time."

"Not the time, man, not the fucking time." The very last thing I want to think or talk about is Syria. I don't need to relive my first capture while enduring a second.

"Yeah." He drops his head against the wall. "But we all felt it, man. It wasn't an easy choice."

Before I can answer, the cell door slams open and three men walk through. One grabs for each of us, but it'll be through our dead bodies that we let them rape the girl again.

CHAPTER 16
Codie

I keep checking the time. Waiting for what I'm not sure, but it's been four days since Ryder left, and my worry has amplified with every passing sunset.

His sister, Hayes, has called me at least twice a day to chat. I like her well enough, but she talks a lot. From what she's said, I realize Ryder's told her how fucked up I am. Maybe in a nicer way, but she knows all the same.

The sound of slamming doors has me pushing the chair back from my table where I'd been eating dinner and rushing to the door.

"One, two, three," I whisper as each lock disengages. The door opens, and all the air in my lungs whooshes out as I see two men walking up my driveway. "No," I gasp, feeling my legs weaken.

"Whoa there, hang on, Codie." Theo grabs me before I crash to the ground. "Deep breaths. Take a minute."

"Is he…" I can't even say it.

Staring at Nix in the illumination of the porch light, his hard mask doesn't give me hope. "He's not," the big man confirms as Theo walks me over to the couch.

"So, what's going on then?" I look between them, hoping for an easy answer, knowing I'm going to get a heart-breaking one.

Nix is the one to grab my hands in his and offer comfort as he speaks. "He was captured alongside Foster and the woman we were sent in to retrieve." My world tilts on its axis, and I suddenly can't breathe.

"We got him out," Theo is quick to reassure, and my head stops spinning.

"But he's in the hospital," Nix replies immediately. "It's not bad; he's been worse. He asked us to come and tell you what's going on." His stare implores me to understand what he's saying.

"Is this because of me?" Horror spreads through me like wildfire. I don't think I could live with myself if I'm the reason Ryder and two more people were captured.

Theo remains quiet, and Nix's head drops to his chest. I guess I have my answer. It's crushing knowing I caused all of this pain.

"It's not because of you, Codie. Christ." Nix drags a hand down his face before looking at me again. "I'm sorry I made you feel like that. Theo has been kicking my ass for days, and Ryder, well, I'd let him."

"Then I don't understand what the look was about." I hate this confusion.

"I know you've been working on getting past your fears of the world. And from what I hear, you've been doing one hell of a bang-up job. But Codie, Ryder could use you. At his side," Nix explains, and I understand now.

"Let's go." My words are stronger than my emotions right now, and I'm not entirely certain I'll be able to do it, but for Ryder, I have to try with every ounce of strength I have in me.

They share a look of doubt. "Are you sure?" Theo asks.

"I'm not. Even a little bit. But I took what you said to heart, Nix. I don't want to be the reason Ryder, or any of you, is hurt. I also don't want to let Ryder out of my life so easily. He's part of me, and I can't lose that." My lip wobbles at just the thought.

"Christ, girl. Come here." Nix keeps shocking me as he pulls me into his chest and rubs my back, offering more comfort than I thought was possible from the man.

Stepping away from him, I gaze between the two men and ask, "Either of you have a tranquilizer?" I'm only half kidding, and I can see they aren't sure whether to laugh or go find one.

"Umm, not here, but I could get one?" Theo offers with a smirk. I have no doubt he probably could.

Shaking my head, I turn to grab a few things from my desk. "Just let me get a couple of things. Does he need anything from his house? Maybe one of you could go grab it while I compose myself?"

"Already got it." Nix shrugs at my quizzical look. "Figured if you agreed to come, we shouldn't leave too much to chance and give you time to back out. So, hurry the hell up."

"Right. Smart," I respond as I round-up my phone and a pair of headphones. Running up to my bathroom, I grab my anti-anxiety meds and pop one into my mouth. They usually knock me out, but I have a feeling I'll be too amped up this time for them to do that. Hence the music. It will help calm and focus me.

Jogging back down the stairs, I see both Ryder's friends standing by the open front door and it hits me then, I'm not just stepping outside, feeling the air, seeing the world. I'm leaving the property. I'm going to a place I've never seen or been to, and I can feel my heartrate accelerating already. My breathing grows heavy, and stars dance in front of my eyes.

"If I pass out, just carry me," I huff out.

Both men grab an arm and slowly help me out of the house. The moon is blinding as I walk past the front porch, around the garage, and to the truck in the driveway.

"I can't breathe," I murmur. My chest is tightening exponentially.

"Relax, slow breaths," Theo encourages. "Think of Ryder, Codie. He needs you. You'll be with him soon."

I feel sluggish as he picks me up and climbs in the back seat with me. "Close your eyes. Concentrate on the rise and fall of your chest. That's a girl. Keep going." The lazy cadence of his voice helps soothe me as my medication kicks in, and my body slowly slides into a relaxed state.

Slipping the earbuds in my ears, I hit play on a random station. The beat of Adele's "Rolling in the Deep" rushes through my ears, and I relax into the sounds of her words. The strength and endurance behind her message.

I can feel the tires rolling under the truck, the rumble of the soft engine. Movement as we stop and go. The heat from Theo's body as he stares at me while Nix drives.

It doesn't take long for my mind to completely drift and soon, I'm aware but floating free from my body. The fear is left behind, replaced with absolute resolution that I need to be strong for Ryder. That even though he's my rock, I can, and will, regain the power over my life while he's by my side.

Ryder

"Brace for cover!" I yell at Foster and Everett as I see our team coming through the cover of night with a big fucking rocket launcher aimed at one of the shacks beside us.

The buzzing as it's fired and subsequent boom make my ears ring, and the heat of the explosion nearly sears my skin, if not for the walls of our own prison. "Jesus!" Foster grumbles as he picks Ev up in his arms.

It's been two days, and she refuses to speak to either of us. She'll barely sustain eye contact, and I wonder if she's going to make it back home. "Here comes another!" We drop to the ground, covering Everett's body with our own. Ensuring the impact of any debris doesn't touch her is our main objective.

"Go, go, go!" I hear Nix yell outside as groundfire is used as cover for whoever is coming to our shack.

"Here we go, boys!" Weston yells as he shoots the lock off the door.

"Gun!" I shout over the sounds of war breaking out. "Chaos has the girl. Let's cover him." I don't care that I can

barely walk after taking the majority of the beatings these sons of bitches liked to deliver. A dislocated knee is the least of our worries at this point.

Thankfully, we all have enough training to know how to deal with dislocations. Doesn't mean the pain has lessened. Especially with a bullet wound to my shoulder. I'm confident I've got infection rushing through my blood, too.

"Up and over guys, up and over," Wes instructs as we come out guns ablaze. Foster runs with the girl in his arms, and Theo helps him up the wall with her. Both landing and likely running.

"Your turn, Tac." Fuck.

"You first." I nod towards where Foster and Everett just were. "They need all the help they can get." He's skeptical at first, but nods when I hit him with a hard glare.

"See you soon." I lay down cover fire with Nix as Wes runs and follows after Foster. Theo sits up on the wall, his rifle aimed at any moving target he can find before he fires another round.

"Let's go, Tac!" Nix yells, and I can only pray my knee holds me up. Pushing away from the shack wall, I feel the heat of bullets flying past me as I maneuver over to where Nix is taking cover behind some oil drums.

"What the fuck did they do to you?" He growls as I land in a heap at his feet.

"They're creative." I stare up at Theo as I see rage cover

his face moments before he blasts the compound with another grenade.

"Let's get you home." Nix curses as he helps me to my feet. Climbing the rope up the wall is not nearly as easy as the last time. I can feel my adrenaline waning, and the blood rushes through me at rapid speed as I get dizzy looking down the other side.

"Might not make it, sir," I mumble as darkness takes me over, and I'm free-falling to the other side before anyone can catch me.

My last thought is of Codie and who's going to take care of her now.

Jolted awake by movement beside me, I'm surprised to see the woman I've kept thinking of lying beside me. In the hospital. Out of her house.

"What the hell?" I murmur quietly so as not to wake her up.

"She insisted," Nix says from a corner of the room I hadn't seen him in. Pain radiates through me as I try to sit up straighter. "At ease, Tac."

"Thanks. Why would she insist on coming?" It's hard to believe. Codie is only just able to get outside her door now.

"Because you were right about her, man, and I was an ass. Love is a powerful motivator." *Love?*

"We're not there yet." I'm getting there, but I've been

holding back. I know she has, too. We've both been through too much to simply let love happen.

He shrugs. "Maybe you two don't see it, but I'm not blind, Tac. Why do you think I pushed her so hard? If she's not willing to fight for you, she doesn't deserve you." Shocked, I'm speechless. "I knew if she didn't come today, there was no future for you two. But this one, she's a persistent girl. Even in the middle of a breakdown, her mind was fighting her to let go, to let her heart take the lead."

"Is she drugged?" I know her meds knock her out quickly.

"She took an anti-anxiety pill before we left, but she fought through the fog and remained pretty alert. I had to carry her in here. Almost got arrested for that one." He chuckles as he stands and walks over to where I lay holding Codie in my arms. "She was scared. But she fought through a lot of demons, man. Don't let her go."

Gazing down at the woman who is unequivocally the biggest contradiction I've ever seen, I know I won't. "She's stuck with me."

"We good, man?" My boss, mentor, and friend appears worried.

"We're good, Nix."

He leaves, and I'm left in the quiet to digest the past few days. My feelings about Codie. How the mission went down and if there's one thing I'm certain of, it's that this is the life I want.

Missions can be dangerous; they can be the reason I don't come home. But if it means rescuing more people like Everett Gaines, freeing them from hell, I'll do it with my dying breath. Seeing Codie here now, I believe, more than ever, that while she might not think she's strong enough to handle what life throws at her, she can overcome anything.

She battled her darkest demons to be by my side. This girl is a fighter, and I'm eager to prove to her that we're it for each other. She's mine, now, and I won't let her back down.

Codie

I feel the angst building in my bones as I listen to Nix and Ryder talk about me. The meds keep me from being alert enough to elicit a response to what they say. When I hear Nix explain why he did what he did, I want to cry. I also want to punch him right in the chest for making me feel so…useless.

On the same note, I also want to hug him for giving

me the push I needed to become a woman Ryder can be proud to be with. It's been nearly a month since Ryder pushed his way into my life, and I can't feel any type of regret over it. I feel elation and excitement.

I feel a future I never saw myself having after all the turmoil centered around my life. I will always carry the pain of losing Lucas, but now, I can intertwine it with the happiness I reminisce about when I was planning his birth. I remember the first kick, the first time I heard his heartbeat, the first ultrasound, and I can breathe. I can talk about him and not experience the crippling apprehension I once did.

I'm not cured, not by a long shot. But I feel I can function again. At least a little bit more than before. Maybe I'll be able to leave the house without counting my steps, maybe I won't have a panic attack in the driveaway.

"Maybe you can say hello now?" Ryder's soft voice breaks my thoughts, and I stare up at him, happy beyond words that he's alive.

"Hi."

"Your thinking hurts my head." He laughs as I frown.

"Sorry." I smile at him because I know he's teasing me. "I thought I was masking it pretty well."

"Maybe to Nix. Not me." His hand brushes the hair back from my face, and I close my eyes. Savoring the soft touch. "I'm glad you came."

"Me, too," I answer, turning my head to kiss the palm of his hand. "I'm sorry you were hurt." Theo and Nix only gave me the bare minimum of details.

His eyes search mine for a full minute before he responds. "It was worth it."

"Do you think she'll be okay?" I overheard Theo talking on the phone to someone about the woman they rescued, and she was in bad shape.

"Honestly? I think physically she will. Mentally, she's going to need a lot of help." Ryder's eyes sadden at what the woman must have gone through. I can't help but feel for her.

"You should rest," I instruct him.

"Kiss me first." He leans down before I can respond and captures my lips in a slow caress that quickly deepens. I'm lost in the sensations of his mouth as his hands roam my body. I light up for this man, and I can't wait to have him home once again.

CHAPTER 17
Coolie

*A*fter spending all day with Ryder and having only one minor freak out, the doctors and nurses demanded that I go home once visiting hours were over. If not for Ryder insisting that I get some rest and calm down, I would have forced myself to stay. I would have pushed through every apprehension I had. But I could feel my body gearing up for a brutal attack, and I knew I needed to get myself under control before coming back in the morning.

Thankfully, Theo and Nix were around to help me back to my house and understand my limitations. If not for the fact I know I can't control my reactions to the outside world, I would have been embarrassed.

Circumstances made me what I am, and I won't

apologize to anyone for it. Especially people who look upon me with disdain.

"You sure you're okay to go in by yourself?" Theo asks again.

I begged off having either one of them checking through the house. My creeper hasn't been back since Ryder came into my life, and I'm confident I can walk to the door. Plus, I know once I'm inside, I likely won't make it past the front door. I'll need a few moments to decompress from the day, and movement will be slow coming as soon as the door shuts.

"I'm positive. Whoever was bothering me has obviously lost interest." I force a smile that I don't feel as Theo nods.

"Alright, we'll be back in the morning. Call if you need anything." He watches with worry as I walk up to the house.

It feels weird, strolling towards the front door. It's been a long time since I've seen the outside of the structure. It needs new paint.

Grabbing the doorknob, I twist and don't even realize what's wrong until it's too late and the door is closing behind me.

Getting slammed against the wood, I hit my head off one of the deadbolts and immediately feel blood dripping down my cheek. A body holds me roughly against the frame as I try to struggle free. Before I can scream, a sweet scent invades my nostrils, and soon, I'm dizzy and my eyes are rolling into the back of my head.

No. No. No.

Ryder...

Ryder

I felt the excruciating pain Codie was in when she left, and I knew I had to convince her to go home. As much as I enjoyed having her by my side, I recognized it was harming her state of mind. She's so fucking strong but so damn fragile at the same time.

She's slowly coming out of her shell, but I also realize that today, she forced herself to be by my side and that's not good for her psyche.

After being pumped full of more drugs, sleep beckons me with a warm embrace, and soon, I've surrendered to the Sandman. While my body rests, my mind is ablaze with torment.

"Who do you work for?" The man in the mask screams at me again. When they tried to take Everett from Foster's hold, I put up one hell of a fight and forced them to interrogate me instead.

"Your momma." I spit the blood pooling in my mouth on the ground at his feet.

"You'll regret that." He laughs as he brings a pipe across my chest. Pain erupts, and I fight with everything in me to react as little as possible.

The CIA's torture training tactics are coming in handy for the second time in my life. Can't say I'm too pleased about it.

"Who do you work for?" he snaps again, putting pressure on the wound in my shoulder.

"Ahhh," I groan out, feeling the warmth of blood trickle down my arm and drip onto the floor. "Alright." I breathe. "Alright."

He chuckles thinking he's won. "Weak man."

"I'll tell you," I say, inhaling a deep breath. I realize what's coming next. "Once you tell him"—I nod to the man in the corner—"how much you enjoyed banging his sister last night."

Cursing lights up the room, and I laugh at their reactions until the fucking pipe is brought down against my ribs repeatedly, and I'm nearly unconscious.

"Fuck," I hiss as they back off. Coughing, I roll on the floor, trying to protect my vital organs.

"Before we're done, you'll talk. If not, we'll take it out on the girl." Over my dead fucking body they will.

CHAPTER 18

Theo

"Codie!" I bang on the door for the fifth time. I know she's got issues, but fuck, I don't have time for this shit.

"She sleeping maybe?" Nix asks, walking behind me. The fact he hasn't bolted yet shocks me.

"Maybe?" I shrug. But I know enough about her to recognize that she wouldn't just ignore us like this. Not after yesterday.

"You have a key, right?"

"Yeah." I didn't want to just barge into her place, though. Seeing no other options, I pull it out and find that only the doorknob is locked. "Fuck." Taking the Berretta out of my side holster, I slowly open the door, and immediately, I see her purse lying on the ground, and the back door leading into the kitchen is wide open.

"This isn't good," Nix mutters behind me as we go through her entire house in the hopes she's hiding. "Ryder's going to fucking kill us," he says as we enter the front room at the same time.

"More than kill us." Today is going to be a bad fucking day.

Codie

"You killed him, Codie," a voice murmurs in my fogged brain. "He's dead because you're useless." A voice that feels vaguely familiar.

"Who?" I mumble. Or, at least, I think I do.

"You were a deadbeat mom before he even entered the world. You should have died instead of him," It taunts.

Lucas.

I wish every day that it was me instead of him.

"I know," I whisper. Tears immediately spring to my eyes. I'll never forget my failures.

"I should bleed you out, right here, right now. Make you suffer." Why do I know this voice?

Opening my eyes, I'm met with complete darkness, and it only takes a second to realize that I've been blindfolded. Pulling my arms, I can tell my wrists are tied behind my back, and I'm strapped to a chair.

"Why are you doing this?" I get no answer. I can hear my captor moving around, but he remains silent now. "Who are you?" I struggle to get free with no success. Even my legs are bound to the chair.

I hear something being set down on a hard surface, then it's instantly followed by the sounds of a baby crying. The mechanical tone tells me it's some sort of recording, but the impact of what it means is no less.

Lucas.

I never heard his cries. He never got to inhale a breath of air to even try to scream with life. I failed him, and I'm getting my penance now.

The cries grow more frenetic, as though the baby is terrified, and I can only imagine how horrid it must be. How frantic the mother must have been.

At least, she didn't kill her baby.

Not like me.

"You're a baby killer," the voice growls in my ear.

A wracking sob breaks through my body, and I have no way to defend myself because it's true. "I know," I scream out loud. The pain of that day, the remembrance of how heart-breaking it was rushes through me, and as I feel a prick in my arm and sluggishness roll through my body, I'm brought back to the day I wish I'd died instead.

"Do you have a name?" The nurse who has been with me this whole time gazes at me expectantly.

"He was so strong," I say, staring down at his pale cheeks.

"He was." Her caring smile should soothe me.

"I failed you," I profess to my son.

"No dear, you didn't. Sometimes these things just happen." Her hand grips my arm, and I want to scream at her, but my voice is hoarse from the crying I've been doing for almost twenty-four hours.

"I did. He's dead. I'm here. It should have been me." A lone tear drops from my chin and lands in the soft, dark hair dusting his head.

"Oh, Codie. No. God has big plans for this one." I hate the mention of a higher power.

Glaring at her, I hiss, "He's supposed to be faith. He's supposed to be love and light. He wasn't supposed to take my family from me. Not now. Not him."

"What's his name, Codie?"

"Lucas. His name is Lucas Ray, and he was too good for this unforgiving world." Another nurse enters the room, and I know it's time. Time for me to hand him over. To allow my life end. "I'm so sorry, Lucas." Leaning down, I kiss his cold cheek, and for once, I don't pray.

Instead, I curse. And I curse until I have no words left in me.

As they take him from my arms, I know it's time I lock myself away for good. My life is over before it's truly begun, and I won't allow myself the hurt of loss again.

The world is a cold hell I'd rather stay away from.

Ryder

"Say that again?" I glare at Theo and Nix as they stand at the end of my bed. Both of their big bodies poised for action. Likely to hold me down because if I heard them right through the fog from these fucking drugs, they said Codie is missing.

"Codie wasn't at her house this morning. I watched her walk inside last night. Close the door. But now she's missing." Theo explains again.

I'm raging inside. "If I had a gun right now, I'd shoot you both," I roar as I start ripping cords and IV's from my body. The machines start going haywire with noise. "Who's checking the cameras on her house?"

Nurses come running in, but I ignore them and wait

on Nix. "Foster is watching the video. Weston is on his way to her house for evidence that the police may miss."

"Where are my clothes?"

"Mr. Morrison, you need to get back in bed." one nurse demands.

"No," I snap. "I need to find my fucking woman." Pain or not, I'm searching for her. "Is anyone tracking her phone?"

"It was in her purse on the floor," Theo explains as he hands me pants.

Fire races through my leg as I stretch the stitches in my thigh. "Give me your phone." I hold a hand out for one of them.

"Who are you calling?" Nix asks.

"Her fucking parents. I should have done this days ago. I should have done a lot of fucking things." Regret burns an acid hole in my gut.

"Shit." I hear Theo through the ringing of the phone.

"Get the fuck out!" I shout at the nurses as they try to push me back in bed.

"Get him discharge papers. He's leaving." Nix's take no shit tone has them moving.

"Hello?" A feminine voice finally answers.

"Is this…" I blank because I don't remember her fucking name. "Mrs. Ray?"

"Yes, who's this?" she asks back.

"My name is Ryder Morrison. I'm your daughter's

other half." Silence greets me, and my temper flares. "Codie is missing."

"Oh." Her lack of response makes me blink.

"Oh? Are you fucking kidding me? Your child, the one you tossed out like fucking garbage, is missing and all you can say is oh?" Jesus fucking hell.

"I'm sorry, Mr. Morrison, you've caught me by surprise."

"Poor fucking you. Have you even thought about her in the last three years or was she so easily forgettable?" I have a lot of opinions regarding these fucking people, and she's not going to like any of them.

"No, of course not. I just... Codie left, and she wanted nothing to do with me when I tried to reach out. Do...do...the baby, is he missing, too?" I pull the phone away from my ear to look at it, wondering if she's lost her fucking mind.

"Lucas. His name was Lucas. And no, he's not missing, he's dead." I won't sugar coat shit for her.

"Damn," Theo mutters.

"Dead?" Horror and fear finally break through the line.

"He was still-born, Mrs. Ray. But right now, that's not the concern. Codie has had someone harassing her for weeks. I need to know who the fuck in her life before she came here had it out for her."

"Cold, man," Nix says as I slip my shoes on.

Not bothering with a shirt because it'll cause the stitches in my shoulder to rip and the medical staff will try to prevent me from leaving again, I walk out of the room with Nix and Theo hot on my trail.

"Like an enemy?" Is this woman stupid?

"Yes."

"Jason's father came around about a year ago wanting to know where she was. Where the baby was."

"What did you tell him?" I know I'm already going to hate the answer.

"Well, the truth. We have no idea where Codie is. She never told us and hasn't contacted us since she left." There's a tremor in her tone.

"You keep saying she left. Your husband kicked her out because she wouldn't get an abortion. You put her on the streets for six months. She was seven-fucking-teen!"

"I'll regret that till the day I die." I can hear tears in her voice now.

"You fucking better." I hang up before I really lose it and do something I'll regret. "Anything from Chaos or Shaker yet?" The elevator ride down to the parking lot is slow as hell.

"Nothing. Police are canvassing the neighborhood, but there's been no signs of anything. Not many people even know who they're talking about. She's made it easy for this perp," Nix explains, regret in his tone.

He's not wrong. Codie's reclusiveness *has* made it easier to put a target on her back. "I need her phone."

"Okay?" Theo questions.

"Her therapist. I need to talk to her. She might know something," I comment. If anyone knows my girl, it's going to be her.

"I'll text Shaker." Theo pulls out his phone and does just that as the elevator doors finally open. Climbing into Nix's truck, pain rips through my broken body and worry stammers through my heart.

Where the fuck are you, Codie?

CHAPTER 19
Codie

"*P*lease." I wail with a dry throat, making it feel like I'm swallowing pins. "Turn it off." I know this guy's watching me. I can feel his eyes, sometimes his breath, on the back of my neck. He's enjoying my suffering. The constant screams. My eyes are dried to the point they're swollen now because I have nothing left.

I don't know how much time has elapsed since he took me, but it feels like weeks, maybe even months. I don't know if anyone is looking for me, or if they know I'm gone. I'm trapped in this time loop of crippling emotional agony, and I see no end in sight as I try to reason my way out.

The constant infant cries make my ears feel like they're bleeding, and I wish I were deaf. I wish he would do whatever it is he wants done and move on. "Please, make it stop."

"Why? It's not like the baby got to experience life. You should suffer for your failures." The voice is raspy, and I know I recognize it, I just don't know how.

"I'm sorry," I whisper again, licking my cracked lips and praying for water.

"I don't care if you're sorry. You destroyed so many lives with your selfish actions, and then you killed your baby. You deserve everything I plan on doing to you and more." It's there, right at the front of my brain. I know this man. If only the sounds would stop, I could figure it out.

"Water, please," I beg. Maybe if I can get him to keep talking...

"That infant never got water." My head drops to my chest at the truth.

"I know."

"There's no better way for you to suffer than depriving you of everything he missed out on in life. You took it from him." *Who is he?*

"I did." I've never said anything less. I failed Lucas because I was a scared teenage mom who had no idea what she was doing. While it's not an acceptable excuse, it is the truth. I've come to accept it. Accept how it played a major role in not noticing that something was even wrong until it was too late.

"I didn't know. I had no idea there was a problem," I try to explain.

"I don't care!" he screams, and the backhand comes out of nowhere. Pain explodes through my skull, and my blindfold falls off my face.

Blinking into the light rays of the sun, I capture a glimpse of his face for the first time, and it clicks. "Mr. Jones?"

"Don't you Mr. Jones me, baby killer." I flinch at the moniker. I've blamed myself for so long. I was finally beginning to see that there was nothing I could have done to prevent the loss of Lucas' life. But the more he says it, the more my subconscious tries to tell me it's true. It was my fault.

"I'm not." I try valiantly to object to his accusation. "There was nothing that could have been done. Lucas was destined to be with the angels."

"Lucas?" He breaks down. Until I found out I was pregnant, the Jones family had always been so kind to me. They welcomed me with open arms. Jason's grandfather, this man's father, Lucas, is the man I wished was my own dad. Naming my son after someone so selfless and caring seemed fitting to me. Even though he passed months before I became pregnant, and thankfully before he could see how vindictive his own family could be, he was a man that I respected deeply.

"After your father," I whisper, another tear slipping freeing. Sliding down my cheek.

His agonizing cries are the only sounds to be heard in this room I'm held in. I don't even know where I am. But the fear of being outside my home starts to kick in, and I feel the anxiety attack climbing its way up my throat. With the heat of a fire breathing dragon, my esophagus closes, and inhaling becomes difficult.

"I need to go home," I mumble hoarsely. I'm ignored, and I have to close my eyes and count in order to think properly. "One," I inhale. "Two," I exhale. "Three." Ryder, where are you?

It's an unfair thought. He likely has no idea I'm missing. I can't count on anyone to come to my rescue but me. I have to be my own savior in this chapter of my story, or I'll never make it out of here alive.

Ryder

"Well?" I gaze around the room, it's been a full forty-eight hours since Codie has gone missing. Four computer screens blaze in front of me, and none of us have a fucking clue where her ex's father disappeared to after his wife killed herself upon hearing about the death of the baby six months ago. "There's nothing?" A man can't just ghost off the earth like that.

"Look, Ry, man," Theo starts and glances to Foster and Weston before he continues. "You need to stop thinking like the boyfriend and remember why you were chosen for this team."

"What are you talking about?"

Nix watches us from his office while making phone calls and pulling all the favors he can.

"Your computer skills, man. You created an entire secure network just for this team. Use that. Use what you have and track this son of a bitch down like the dog he is," Foster tells me.

"Shit." They're right. My emotions are getting in the way of discovering the information that we need to find Codie. "Alright." I have to get the thoughts about what could possibly be happening to her out of my head and treat this like any other operation.

She's the target we have to find, and that's it.

"You got this, man." Wes smacks my shoulder from his seat next to me. I ignore the searing pain of the movement from the shot in my shoulder and power through. Codie is counting on me to remain objective enough to find her.

Opening the server, I search the man's name and all properties he's owned over his lifetime. Discovering only three, I first verify the new owners and then move onto his deceased wife's name. Nothing stands out for her, either. Only thing she's ever owned that didn't have both their names on it is an old car.

I have to think outside the box.

His parents.

A search in the mother's name yields nothing. The father, however, shows four houses, a warehouse, and an old general store. The houses are scattered across the country, and all are occupied or demolished. Only one house is in driving distance, roughly eight hours away in Scranton, Pennsylvania. The warehouse was turned into an apartment complex in Idaho in the seventies. The general store, though, has been abandoned since the late nineties and is in the same town in Pennsylvania as the house.

"I think I've got something," I say as I continue to look for property deeds. The store is still listed in the father's name, but the majority owner is his son. "Scranton, Pennsylvania."

"Shit. He could have driven her there no problem," Foster chimes in.

"He'd have had to shoot her up with something, though. I don't think she would have slept for that long," Theo muses.

"Nix!" I shout.

"Yeah?" He pops his head out of his office.

"Can you get a plane?" No way in hell am I leaving her in his hands for eight hours more.

"On it," he says, going back to his call.

"Are you sure this is where she is, though?" Foster wonders.

"And that it's him?" Theo echoes.

"It's all I've got. There's nowhere else. Jason isn't even in the country, so it can't be him." I fucking hate this.

"Pack your gear! If Tac says that's where she is, that's where she is. Let's go bring her home. Shaker, make sure you have supplies. Chaos, no explosives. Phantom, nothing too big." Foster and Theo walk away mumbling about their orders while Weston rushes to the supply room. "I'd like to tell you to sit this one out, but I know you won't. So do me a favor, let me handle this creep. You get your girl." Nix offers his hand, and I know if I don't agree, he will sideline me.

"Sure. Codie is all I want, anyways."

Nix eyes me critically. "Take a seat, Ryder. You look ready to fall over." I should deny it, deny him. But I'm exhausted. The past few days is catching up to me, and my body isn't nearly as ready as I need it to be.

"Yeah, sure," I agree as my frame drops into the chair beside me without permission. I need rest, but that's not going to happen without Codie. I need her safe and with me more than anything else, and there isn't a soul who will convince me otherwise.

Pulling out my phone, I scroll through a few photos I took of Codie when she was sleeping. Some when she wasn't looking and a couple of us together. The sounds of my friends—my team—gearing up to help me save her is comforting but not nearly as much as physically being with her. The photos will hold me together when all I want to do is blow everyone off. Go after her myself.

"Plane's ready!" Nix shouts as they all come carrying bags full of gear that we may or may not need to rescue her.

"Come on, man." Theo grips my elbow, helping me to my feet as we load into the elevator and head back down to the trucks.

Forcing my body to move forward, I prepare for the flight ahead and subsequent battle that could ensue. Jones is one man. How much damage could he possibly inflict on us?

Codie

I float in and out of consciousness as I wait on death or rescue. My heart races out of control so often, I'm terrified it's going to beat right out of my chest.

My time on this earth is coming to an end, and I have so many regrets. More than what's healthy. The most significant being that I shut down after losing Lucas. I did him a great disservice by allowing the pain of his loss to defeat me.

Instead of celebrating the joy he brought to my life for a few short months, I cowered and ran away. I didn't confront my parents about their treatment of me. I didn't tell Jason what happened to his son. I didn't healthily grieve for my boy. I let it become my excuse to close myself off and never allow anyone else into my heart again.

Until Ryder Morrison.

A man of so many convictions and good intentions. A man worthy of the world and a woman who doesn't fall apart because she's scared.

But lord have mercy, I want him. I want so much more with Ryder than we were granted. I want to be able to be the woman he desires without question.

"Mr. Jones?" I try calling. My voice is a hoarse whisper that can barely be heard, though. "Please let me go."

The blindfold was replaced after I was drugged, and I can't see anything once again. Being left in the dark is working in my favor, however. I don't have time to obsess over my surroundings.

"I don't deserve this!" I call out louder.

"And Allison did?" he snarls in my ear, his hot breath burning my flesh. Shivers race up and down my spine as he shakes the chair I'm sitting in violently. Infant wails still play in the background.

"No. None of us do," I cry out.

"You do!" he screams, and I flinch away. "Jason won't even come home!" His anger radiates like an inferno, and I feel it to my core. "He says he can't bear the memories of his mom, of what you caused."

"I didn't do anything." I know reasoning with him is impossible. "I was seventeen. I was just as scared as him, but I didn't have anyone to help me. I dealt with the heartache and loss on my own. I had the attachment to Lucas, not any of you!" My temper flares. "You all wanted me to abort my son!"

I no longer care what he does to me. I refuse to shoulder the blame of the death of a woman who wanted nothing to do with her grandchild. He can't hang this over my head. They made their choices, and Lucas and I were never part of them.

"If you had just kept your legs closed, this wouldn't even be a problem." His vicious snarl takes me back.

"Me? What about Jason? He was the one who wanted to! I wasn't ready!"

"Are you saying he raped you?" This man is unhinged.

"No! I'm saying Jason put pressure on me. I was scared, my parents were uncaring. I only wanted to be loved." I hate how much I'm being forced to relive a past I'd much rather move on from.

There's a shift in the air. A deadly presence I can't see but most certainly feel. I try to concentrate on the sounds around me when I feel the cold steel of a blade against my throat. Terror strikes me, and I freeze. My heart pulses and stops. I can't think straight, and before I can even try to beg for my life, Mr. Jones murmurs in my ear, "Say hello to Allison," as I feel the blade dig into my neck and drops of blood trickle down my throat to my chest.

Tears pour down my cheeks as I realize this is the end.

CHAPTER 20

Ryder

*a*fter sleeping on the flight into Scranton, I feel better and more able to tackle the most important part of our mission. "You sure you're good?" Theo asks for the fifth time since landing as we pull up a few blocks from the store we believe Codie is being held in.

"I'm fine, Phantom, and if you ask me once more, I'm going to shoot you in the foot." We alerted the police to what we're doing here, and they're sending a SWAT team to assist, but I'm not waiting, and neither is my team.

Set out in a dead part of town, there's isn't much fear of bystanders getting in the way, so we move forward as one unit. "Two heat signatures in the building," Weston relays from his position a block up with Nix.

"Tac, Phantom, you hold back. Wait for my call," Nix commands as he and Wes move closer. Foster runs ahead with a battering ram to infiltrate the chained front door. "Breach in three, two, one. Go, go, go!"

Foster knocks the door in, Weston tosses in a flash-bang, and they wait until it goes off before entering the building with guns raised, prepared for anything.

"Down!"

"Hands!"

"Drop the knife!"

And I'm off and running. "Fuck, Ryder, wait!" Theo calls out behind me, but soon he's beside me as we enter the building.

Sirens can be heard blaring in the distance, but all I see is Codie...

Blindfolded.

Tied to a chair.

A huge bruise on her cheek.

Blood dripping from a cut in her neck.

Slowly maneuvering my way over to her, I drop to the ground as I reach for the mask over her eyes. "Dove?" I whisper, hoping she's with me still. I don't know what I'll do in a world without her.

"Get an ambo," Nix orders as he drags the older man to his feet and hauls him outside.

"Codie." My voice is harder. I can see her chest rising and falling slowly, so I know she's with me. She's alive. But I cannot tell if she's conscious. She moans but doesn't move to waken or let me know she realizes I'm here. "What the fuck did he do to you?"

"Let's get her untied," Weston suggests as he pulls a knife from his pocket and starts slicing through the rope holding her hostage to the chair. Rope burns mark her wrists and ankles from her struggling, and my anger is renewed as we gently glide her to lay on the floor.

"This wasn't how it was supposed to be," I murmur into her hair.

"This isn't your fault, man," Wes tries to reassure.

"But it is. I should have kept looking. I shouldn't have become complacent." When I found that her ex was out of the country, I didn't imagine the father was the one after her. I never would have guessed that.

"This dirty son of a bitch." Theo comes storming back into the room. "Says it's her fault that his wife killed herself. Fucking weak bastard."

"What?" I roar. Standing, I leave Codie in the care of Wes as I go looking for Ben Jones. "Hey!" I snap as I come up on Nix holding him against the bumper of our SUV that Foster must have brought over.

"What?" Ben groans.

"Why? Why the fuck did you come after her?" I need to hear it from his mouth.

"She made my son leave. My wife killed herself when she found out the baby was dead." He spits on the ground. "It should be her buried, not my wife."

Disbelief renders me mute. "You guys pushed her away. Tossed money at her to have an abortion. She did what she could with the path she was pushed onto. None of this is on her shoulders. You're the man. Where the fuck was your integrity?" Pushing into him, I crowd his body into the glass until he has nowhere else to go.

"Whatever," he mutters.

"You didn't even teach your son to be a man. Take care of his responsibilities. But that's okay. I'm man enough to own up to them for you both. I'll take care of her. I'll nurture the few memories she has of a son who was too good for the likes of you deadbeats." Walking away, I'm more determined than ever to break Codie out of her shell and show her the world isn't such a bad place to be when you have the right people on your side.

With the police and ambulance rolling in, I know I don't have much time before Codie is taken to a local hospital, and she's going to need me every step of the way. Entering the building, I see Weston is trying to coax her awake with a cool cloth on her neck and cheeks. Paramedics rush in once they arrive and take over the scene.

Standing on the sidelines isn't in my forte, but I wait until they give me the all clear to come in closer because my own strength is waning, and I'd rather not be the patient again.

"Hey, man, you all right?" Theo asks as they load Codie on a stretcher. I can hear Nix barking orders outside, so I know he's got the police handled.

"Yeah. I'm fine," I tell him as the medics start rolling Codie out. "I'll see you there."

"Son of a bitch should be charged federally," Nix barks at some guy in a suit. Probably a high-ranking cop.

"Listen, we need to investigate. I asked you to wait on SWAT," the man retorts.

"And I told you a girl's life was at risk, and that she was taken across state lines. That makes this federal. That means this is mine, and I'll do with him as I please." Nix snaps back and steps into the guy's personal space. If I weren't so exhausted, I'd be laughing at his expense.

"Commander!" I yell. He looks at me with a quirked eyebrow. "Give Asher McCall a ring. I'm sure he'll happily deal with this. You know he loves paperwork." Asher is our contact at the Department of Justice who often deals with situations such as this, where law enforcement doesn't need to know exactly what it is that we do.

Nix smirks as he pulls out his phone. McCall will be here in an hour. Two tops.

Climbing in the ambulance with Codie, I hold her hand as we roll out, and for the first time in years, I fucking pray this entire experience hasn't set her back from all the hard work she's put in to this point.

Codie

Beep. Beep. Beep.

I know those sounds.

Nothing good comes from them.

Fear, pain, annoyance, they all roll through me with the speed of a lightning bolt. With the destruction of one, too.

I should be panicking. I'm obviously not at home. Or anywhere I actually want to be, but I'm feeling light. High.

The last thing I remember is a cold blade at my neck, and my entire body tenses as I wonder if I'm dead. Maybe that's why I'm not flipping out like I normally would be.

Reaching up with a free hand, I feel a small bandage on my neck, and the pressure of poking at it causes pain, so I'm not dead. I'm very much alive.

Chancing to open my eyes, the room is dimly lit, and as I search the room, I see Ryder asleep in a chair in one corner with an older couple standing and talking outside the window above him. Doctors, nurses, and visiting people walk by with no idea that my world is shifting.

The paralyzing fear I've been so consumed with for years is absent. Or at the very least, put on the back burner. I don't have the usual tunnel vision, and I can breathe without restraint.

"Knock, knock." The door slowly opens and in walks my therapist, Amy. "Oh, hi, Codie. I wasn't expecting you to be awake yet." Her voice is hushed as Ryder sleeps on.

"What's going on?" I whisper the question.

"Well, it's been about two days since you were brought in. Only one since Ryder had you transferred to Charleston." I watch her expectantly. The woman is smart. She knows what I'm asking and sits on the bed next to me, even though this is the first time we've met face to face. We've had plenty of Skype sessions, so I don't feel like she's a stranger. "I owe you a huge apology, Codie."

I'm confused. "I don't understand."

"That first time we talked two years ago, I never once considered you had a chemical imbalance from postpartum depression. I should have, and I feel horrible I didn't." She shakes her head, and I remain silent. "Your crippling fear of the outside world was very real. And I tried my best to understand all your fears and anxieties. What I should have been focusing on was your loss."

Looking down, I shrug. I don't know where she's going with this, but I doubt I'd have been easily fixed at any point before now.

"You didn't just lose Lucas, Codie. You lost your parents, your boyfriend. A family that until you became pregnant, had become your own."

"What are you saying?"

"I'm saying," she sighs. "I misdiagnosed you with borderline agoraphobia. While I believe there is some of that in there, I don't believe it's the underlying problem to your mental state."

"So, what is?" I half laugh because what else could it be?

"Fear, Codie. With a good mix of postpartum depression."

"Fear? How can fear make me unable to leave my

house?" I snort, completely skeptical of what she's saying.

"Because," Ryder's voice breaks the silence as he walks over. "You were so afraid of letting yourself feel anything again, it was easier to lock yourself away and forget what it felt like to live again." He sits on the bed on the opposite side of Amy and cups my jaw in his hand. Turning my tear-filled eyes to look at him. "God, dove. You were hurt so damn bad. Worse than anyone should ever be. You were rejected by every fucking person in your life."

"Right," I respond. "Needed that reminder." Let's not forget that one of those people also kidnapped and tried to kill me.

"No, dove. You don't. But to move on, you need to be able to count on people again. You need someone in your life who is going to show you what it's like to live and be happy." His feelings are more than transparent in his tone as he leans forward, laying a light kiss on my lips.

The damn breaks and all the pain, the heartache, the agony of losing my entire life and locking myself away for nearly three years breaks free and huge, pain-filled sobs burst from my heart.

The rejection.

The loss.

The heartache.

It's all real. It's here. A living, breathing beast inside my body, and I can't slow down the projection of pictures that enter my mind as each shattering memory plays like a sad movie.

"Oh god," I scream into the room, releasing my agony. Purging the demons from my body as Ryder holds my weakened frame.

"I've got you, dove. I'm here. I'm not going anywhere." His words are whispered in my ear as people rush into the room.

"Codie," Amy calls my name, and it sounds like it's coming through a tunnel again. "I'm going to give you a very light sedative. Nothing to put you to sleep, but just enough to calm you down, okay?"

The weight of the world is crushing my chest and taking a breath proves difficult as I try to tell her yes. Nodding instead, I cling to Ryder like the lifeline he has become.

"Please don't leave me," I beg of him.

"Not happening." Pushing me back into the bed, he lays down beside me as the medication pours through my bloodstream like a lazy creek on a Sunday morning after a light rainfall.

"Codie, these are Ryder's parents, Eric and Andrea Morrison." Amy points to the older couple I'd observed over Ryder's sleeping form when I first woke up. "They're going to be in town for a couple of weeks or until Hayes goes into labor." My brain is becoming too foggy to understand why they need to be here.

"Why?" My question is blunt, but Amy grins at me anyways, knowing full-well why.

"They want to get to know you. They also want to reassure you that even when Ryder is gone for work, they're here for you, too."

"Oh." My eyelids are growing heavy, and I can feel myself falling into a state of ambiguity. With so much happening around me, I genuinely need time to reflect on the changes.

With the mix of exhaustion and the sedative, I find myself ready for sleep again. "Sleep, dove. I'll be here watching over you," Ryder whispers into my neck, and I'm secure in the knowledge that he'll be here when I need him.

CHAPTER 21

Ryder

$\mathscr{H}$olding Codie through the night, pushing her nightmares out of her mind, is the greatest honor I've ever been given. Through this entire ordeal the past four days, Amy and I have gotten to know each other quite well. She's given me insight into what's happening in the darkest corners of Codie's mind so I can help her heal and move forward with her life.

First and foremost is closure. Codie was able to bury Lucas. She gave him all the love she could at the time, but we both agree, she has some lingering feelings she needs to expel. I've already booked us a flight to South Dakota next week. Once she's strong enough to leave the hospital.

Even though Codie has been lightly sedated, she still suffers with some anxiety. After a long talk with her last night when she woke from a bad dream, she confessed that with what Amy said about her hiding from being hurt again, the idea of going out into the world doesn't seem nearly as terrifying.

"Now listen here, mister. That is my child in there, and I am damn well going to see her." A shrewd voice breaks the silence of the early morning, and while Codie moves, she doesn't wake as I climb out of the bed I've been sharing with her.

The stitches in my leg and shoulder pull as I move gingerly after being resewn when we got here. Stepping softly, I open the door a crack and slip out, pulling it shut behind me. "Can I help you?" I glare at the man and woman I suspect are Codie's parents.

"I'm trying to see my daughter," she huffs.

"And you are…" I let the question hang.

"Maya and Clark Ray. We received a phone call three days ago that she was brought in." Fucking Theo. I told him not to call them. Shit stirrer that one.

"I'm Ryder Morrison—"

"The rude man who called me?" Maya interrupts before I can say anything else.

"If by rude, you mean the man who cares about Codie, rescued her, and is currently making sure she gets what she needs to heal, then yeah, I'm the rude man." Clark remains silent as his gaze watches the door I'm blocking.

"Can we see her, please?" Maya smarts off.

"No," I tell her, crossing my arms over my chest. "She's sleeping right now."

"Jason's father did this?" Clark finally speaks.

"Yeah, he did." My glare doesn't lessen. I have no respect for these people and what they did. I won't allow them anywhere near Codie unless she directly asks for it. "He blames Codie for the suicide of his wife when she found out Lucas was still-born."

"You say his name like he was alive," Clark observes. Not in a malicious or mean manner, but shocked. He's surprised.

"He was very much alive in Codie's body. In her heart. He's alive in her memories. Speaking of him as just a fetus will only break her spirit."

"I understand." He nods, tears hover in his eyes as his wife moves in closer to him, wrapping an arm around his waist.

"Why are you here?" My question is direct because I don't want to mess around.

Maya shocks me with her words. "We screwed up. We pushed Codie out the door and didn't offer comfort and support when she needed it most. We always thought our daughter was out here with her baby just living." She looks at the door. "I had no idea she was hurting so bad."

I'm not satisfied with their answers. I'm not sure I ever will be. I can't imagine my parents throwing me away quite like these two did to Codie, so granting them something I have no hopes in understanding is impossible.

"Come back around lunch. I'll ask her if she wants to see you." Turning, I enter Codie's room again, not giving either of them a chance to say anything.

"Ryder?" Codie's soft voice drags me to her bedside as she gazes up at me with clear eyes.

"Hi, dove," I coo, running a finger down her cheek and along her jaw. Her soft flesh begs to be kissed. Leaning forward, I lay light pecks along her neck, up to her jaw, and seize her mouth with an intoxicating exploration.

Licking her lips, I suck the bottom one into my mouth before cupping the back of her head and hauling her up and into my lap. I could spend hours just kissing Codie as she moans her delight. Tangling our tongues together in a soft duel for more.

"When can I go home?" She pulls back breathless. But I can't stop tasting her. I'm desperate for more of her sweet flavor.

"Soon," I growl into her ear as I suck the lobe into my mouth. Pushing her back onto the bed, I lay over her, hands touching anywhere they can reach as she yanks my shirt up my back and pulls me closer.

Digging her nails into my shoulder blades, she scores them down my flesh, leaving what I'm sure are red marks that I'll be dying to see later. "Codie," I hiss out. "Don't do that." She presses her naked pussy into my hard ridge and rubs back and forth.

"I need you, Ryder," she whines quietly into the room. Her legs wrapping around my hips to drag me in closer to her heated core only makes it harder to say no. "Please, Ryder."

"Fuck, woman. The things I'd like to do to you." Slipping one hand between us, I trail down her body and find her warmth. "There she is." Rubbing gently between her folds, I have to place a hand over Codie's mouth to keep her moans quiet as I rub her into completion.

"Mmmm." She humps into my hand as I slip a digit in her tight heat.

"That's it, dove. Come all over my hand. Give it to me, baby." Biting her neck, I can feel myself wanting to let go as she clenches on my fingers and cries into my hand as her body shivers and shakes out her orgasm.

Lifting my hand from her mouth, I lean up on my

elbow and bring up my fingers that were just buried in her sweetness and suck her juices off. Her gasp of surprise is adorable. In so many ways, Codie is still completely innocent.

"Let's get you in the shower, then we'll talk to the doctors about getting home soon." I grin as she nods, reluctant to leave the bed in her languid state.

Codie

Warm water hits my back and eases the stiffness from sleeping in hard hospital beds for so long, relaxing me as I beg Ryder to join me. "Please?" I pout.

The man is steadfast in his desire to help me that he forgets I want to be as close to him as he does me. I want to experience life with him, and he's making it difficult.

I don't know everything that happened on his last mission and the details surrounding his injuries, but I do know he risked his life further by coming for me when I needed him most.

"You don't need me in there, dove." He grins, but I

see him wavering as I run my hands up my breasts and into my hair under the pretense of making sure I get it all wet. "Christ, woman," he groans out as his hands begin unbuttoning his pants.

I step back to make room for him, and as soon as he clears the curtain, I wrap my arms around his waist, holding him close. Pressing my breasts into his body, I place my ear against his heart and listen to each beat. Saying a prayer of thanks that I still get a chance to tell him how I feel.

Leaning his head on mine, we stand under the warm spray and just enjoy each other until I feel a pulsing deep inside my body with the need to have him inside of me. My desire for this man has ramped up since facing death. I know can't hide from my feelings any longer, and if I'm indeed going to embrace life, I need to start by being honest with myself.

Kissing his heart, I slowly work my way down his chest to the tiny barbell piercings in his nipples. I suck one into my mouth and feel an answering pulse in his dick as it jumps against my belly. Smiling up at him, I do the same to the other, the smooth metal a welcome relief on my tongue.

Moving down his chest, I dip my tongue into his belly button, nip at his hip until finally, I'm on my knees. His hardened member stares me in the face.

Gazing up at him through hooded eyes, I see him biting his lip, and I know he won't ask for what he wants, but he's damn well praying I'll give it to him anyways.

Leaning forward, I rub my cheek along his length, loving the feel of him. His flesh is soft, but he's hard as a rod. Kissing the tip, I lick along the slit and waste no time sucking him to the back of my throat. Gagging a little when I go too far, his hands thread through my hair as he pulls me back with a warning look for me to calm down.

I love that most about him, I think. The way he's always taking care of me. Even on the cusp of pleasure, Ryder puts me first.

Closing my eyes, I work his length in and out of my mouth slowly, feeling the large vein along his shaft pulsing with each inhale. The way his fists tighten and release in my hair tells me just what he likes most.

Taking him as deep as I can, I swallow around the head of him, and his long groan followed by the tensing of nearly every muscle in his body tells me he's oh so close to releasing his pleasure.

Cupping his balls with one hand, I grip his shaft with the other and slowly slide his flesh up and down. With the head just inside my mouth, more pre-come drips on my tongue, and I enjoy the saltiness of his flavor.

Meeting his lust-filled stare, I tug my hand lightly and say to him, "Ryder, I think..." I pause, suddenly being unsure of my words.

"What? You think what?" he groans, the veins in his neck pumping with each beat of his heart.

"I think I love you."

Time freezes.

I pause, wondering if now is the right time.

"Jesus," he hisses. Picking me up, Ryder grips my hips as he slams his aching cock into my core. "Fuck, dove, you can't do that to a man on the edge of insanity."

"I'm sorry," I whimper as he slowly drags his dick in and out of my pussy.

"No," he barks, thrusting back inside. My head hits the wall as ecstasy pulls me into another universe. "I love you, too."

Everything in me submits to the sweetest words I've ever heard. I could cry with how full my heart is.

"You don't get to take them back," Ryder growls, mistaking the meaning of my tears.

"Never. I'll never take them back," I vow.

"Good. Because you're mine. I won't ever let you go." His lips smash down over mine, and his tongue fucks my mouth in the same manner his cock is taking over my cunt. I can't breathe. I can't move.

I don't want to.

I want everything that we share to be just like this.

Rough.

Harsh.

Soft and sweet.

This is us.

CHAPTER 22
Coolie

Inhale. One.
    Exhale. Two.
Three.

I'm home. For the first time in three years, I'm back in Rapid City, and I'm not sure how I feel about it.

I came to see Lucas. My light in a dark world that I've struggled to let go of since becoming part of the universe again and not just existing within it. Ryder has been a godsend the past week. Allowing me to have space when I need it. A shoulder to cry on when I'm overwhelmed.

The new medications I'm now taking make it easier to breathe in a reality where I can barely find my footing most days. Letting go of the fear that I'm not good enough isn't over, but I'm learning to work through it.

"You're sure you don't want me to come?" Ryder asks as we pull up to the cemetery where Lucas was laid to rest.

Staring out over the grass and trees to the tiny angel headstone that I spent all the money I had on at the time, I know I have to do this alone. "Yeah. I'll be okay." I smile to reassure him as I slowly walk forward, still counting my steps.

Stopping behind the stone before I read the inscription, I take a deep breath in the chilly mountain air. His grave overlooks a valley below the mountain, providing me with a calm I desperately need.

"Hi, baby boy," I murmur, stepping around and seeing his name for the first time in far longer than I like to admit. Sitting down in the dewy grass, I trace the letters with a finger. "I'm sorry I've been gone for so long."

My head hangs in shame. I hate how much I've failed his legacy. "I miss you. Every day I feel your loss in my entire being." Tears hover on my lids. "I wish I'd been able to watch you grow up. Help you take your first steps. Listen to your infant babble. Wake up in the middle of the night to your cries."

Running my fingers through the grass, I close my eyes and pretend I'm back at that hospital again. I speak to him all the things I should have said then but was too grief-stricken to acknowledge.

"I know, now, that you were given to me to test my strength. To make me a better person. We had a few short months together that I will cherish until my dying breath, Lucas." A sob tries to break free, but I force it down. "I need you to know that I wanted you so badly. I want you to know how much I love you. How much I think of you."

Tears flow freely down my face, now. "You were such a surprise to me and your father, Jason. We were young and immature." I wipe a tear before it drops. "I don't blame him for what happened or your loss. I used to blame myself. For so long, I shouldered the blame to a tragedy I never had control over.

"Over the years, I closed myself off. I became this woman I didn't recognize. I sunk into this deep depression I couldn't figure a way out of." Sucking in a deep breath, I notice Ryder watching me as he leans against the rental car. His sister, Hayes, told me of a time when she had been doing this exact same thing, only it was over Ryder's grave, and I now feel closer to her than I ever thought I would allow myself.

"I miss you, Lucas, and I hope one day I'll get to hold you again. I hope one day I'll get to kiss you goodnight and tell you all about the journey I'm about to embark on with Ryder Morrison." The man in question grins sexily at me like he knows I'm talking about him. "I hate that I lost you, son, but I fear if I hadn't, I never would have met Ryder. Or maybe I would have. Who knows? But I have a feeling no matter the outcome of our lives, he would have loved you every bit as much as if you were his boy."

With a fortifying inhale and a clear mind, the pain in my heart eases as I stand. "I love you, Lucas. I always will. I hope that wherever you are, you're at ease." Placing a kiss on my fingers, I lay them lightly on the forehead of the angel and the pressure of not being enough frees me from my past.

I can move on now. Not without Lucas, but with him in my heart as a memory of love and loss. He'll be my angel, and I'll show him that I can live for the both of us now.

Walking right into Ryder's arms, he cradles me to his chest as my tears flow freely. "He'd be proud of you, dove. So damn proud."

"I hope so," I whisper into his chest.

Ryder

Fuck am I in awe of this woman of mine. She's pushed and pulled since leaving the hospital. Pushing me back so she can find her footing. Pulling me forward so I know she's not going anywhere.

It's been a rollercoaster of a week, and I'm glad to be nearly done with it so we can move forward together. The visit to see Lucas was far more emotionally exhausting for Codie, but as soon as she stood up to walk back to me, I saw the heaviness lifting from her shoulders. She no longer held the weight of the world on her small frame, and I couldn't be prouder of her.

I wanted to take her back to the motel we rented for a couple of nights, but she's insisting on going home to see her parents. When they came to the hospital, she hadn't wanted to see them but asked that I tell them we'd see them when we arrived here.

Lucas was the priority. He was who she wanted to see first, and I have to say, it was probably best that she did.

"We don't have to do this, you know." I anticipate there's going to be a confrontation between the small family, and I don't like the idea of Codie feeling less than perfect because of their rejection all those years ago.

"I do." She smiles at me again. "I know it's your first instinct, but you don't have to save me from everything." Her hand cups my cheek as we stop in front of her childhood residence. A home that brought her nothing but pain and heartache. She's so damn strong. Far more than she's ever given herself credit for, and I couldn't be happier to bear witness to it.

"Let's do this." Exiting the car, I walk around to her side where she waits for me to open the door and help her out. It's a small act of chivalry that I quickly learned she enjoys, so I do it as often as I can.

Gripping my hand in her tiny fists, Codie holds my arm in front of her as we walk side by side to the front door of the small bungalow house. The closer we get, the tighter her hold becomes, giving away her anxiety about being here.

"Say the word, and we're gone," I whisper in her ear before she reaches for the doorbell. I know she's pushing herself to do this. Coming back here, ringing the bell of a house that she used to come and go from as she pleased. I hate it, but if there's one thing I've learned over the last week, it's that Codie's as stubborn as Nix.

"I've got this," she tells me as the chime rings through the house.

The door opens, and her mother stands there frozen with shock and fear bright in her blue eyes. "Codie." Her hoarse voice is full of emotion.

"One, two, three." The counting is under her breath so only I can hear it. I leave her be for now. When she explained the numbers and why it was soothing, I no longer considered it as an anxious tick.

It's a coping mechanism brought on by Lucas' birth. She counts the seconds down from the time her dream became a reality, and it helps keep her grounded to life.

"Mother." Codie's tone is a mix of cold greeting and desperation for love.

"Come in, come in." Maya ushers us inside. "I'm glad you came. It's been so long since we've spoken." The rigid stance of Codie's body tells me she's already frustrated with the older woman.

"Over three years." Her voice is hard, and I'm proud of my dove for not skirting around the issue.

Guilt flashes in her mother's eyes, and I almost feel bad for her. "Your father will be down in a few minutes. He's just changing from work." She guides us to the living room before disappearing into what I assume is the kitchen.

"How are you doing, dove?" Wrapping an arm around her waist, I pull Codie into my side as she stares around the room in awe. Photos of her in different stages of her life are hung all around the room like a shrine.

"There were never these many pictures up when I lived here," she comments.

That doesn't surprise me. My own parents don't have this many up of Hayes and me. "You think it's for show?" I don't know what her parents were like before, other than Codie didn't feel as loved as she should have.

"I'm not sure," she whispers as her mother re-enters the room with coffee on a tray.

"Here we go! There's cream and sugar if you like." Maya sits quietly on the chair across from us and stares at the staircase as if willing her husband to come down.

"This is fine, Mrs. Ray, thank you." I break the silence because I want to see her face. I need to get a better read on her when she's not hustling around us. "Codie said you're a teacher?"

She finally brings her head around to look at us. "Oh, yes. I'm just a homeroom teacher now for the high school. I help in the library between classes, as well."

"What happened to your geography class?" Codie asks with a tilt to her head.

"Oh, well, it just wasn't a good fit anymore is all." She smiles, and behind it, I see her own pain. She's trying to push past it and be upbeat, for Codie's sake, I assume. But I recognize her demons. She's haunted by what they did to their only child.

"I see," Codie mutters as she stirs sugar into her coffee, which she doesn't even like.

"Hi there!" Clark booms as he comes into the room, a fake smile on his face, pain in his indifferent stare. "Oh good, you got the coffee, Maya." He leans down to kiss his wife's cheek, and I believe that's the first sincere move I've seen since arriving.

Silence surrounds the room as they all stir coffee that they aren't drinking or smile in the hopes someone else will start a conversation.

So, I do. "Almost four years ago, I was held captive in a cave in a part of the world no decent human being should ever be." Codie's eyes immediately swell with tears because she knows this story. "They had me for a year. Only a couple of months into my captivity, they took each piece of identifying clothing or jewelry I had, put it on someone else and burned the body, so there was no way to distinguish who it was except for my dog tags."

Horror covers their faces. "Good lord," Maya whispers, covering her mouth.

"My family was notified of my death on the same night my little sister was run over and left for dead." To this day the anger over Hayes' accident hasn't vanished. "They lost me hours before they nearly lost Hayes."

"I'm so sorry, Ryder."

"Not your fault, ma'am." I give her a genuine smile because I can tell she knows where I'm going with this. "My point is, my family was given a second chance. It took me two years to come home. It was a full year before I thought I was whole enough to even return after being rescued." I pause a beat because that day is still so fresh in my memory. "My welcoming wasn't completely warm. Hayes was pissed, and I'll tell you, that girl can hold a grudge like no one I know."

"She's okay, after her accident?" Maya's motherly instincts kick in.

"She is. Found herself a real good man, and they're expecting their first baby any day now." I smile thinking of those two. They're disgusting to watch as a couple, but the love they share is one I can foresee for Codie and me. "I can't say I understand what went down in this house three years ago. I can, however, understand what's happening right now. The awkwardness, the need to say sorry, and hopefully forgive, is present in the room, but it's up to the two of you to start."

Staring down at Codie, I see relief and love reflected back at me. Leaning forward I kiss her lightly before addressing her parents again. "Obviously, no one expected to lose Lucas. That sweet boy should have lived a full life. But if your daughter has taught me anything in the few months I've known her, it's that everything happens for a reason. Everything."

"Codie," Clark calls her name softly, and I can feel the emotion emitting off of him as he moves to sit next to his daughter. A girl he should have protected far more than he ever did.

Codie

The rush of tears that break free as my father pulls me into his arms for the first time in three years is swift. The fear from the past invades fiercely and knocks the air from my lungs as he apologizes over and over again.

"I'm so sorry, peanut. We should have done better by you. By our grandson." His typically masculine voice is filled with sadness.

"I wish things would have gone differently," I reply back.

"Me too, Codie. Me too." I don't know how long we hug and cry for, but soon, Momma is worming her way in and taking me from Dad's arms.

"I failed you so much. I don't know how you'll ever forgive me, but I pray to God that one day, you'll have room in your life for us again, Codie. Regret has burned us from the moment we let you walk out that door. Nothing has been the same since that day."

My chin wobbles as I see the toll this has taken on her. The creases of stress and sadness. The frown lines in her forehead and cheeks. She used to smile so much.

"I wish with all of my heart that we could have these years back. I wish everything had been different than it was." I have to stop and swallow. Reaching back for

Ryder's hand, I grip it ardently. "I wish you could have met Lucas. Seen him up close. How beautiful he was."

"Oh, baby." Mom pulls me back in for a tight hug and just like that, it feels like our lost years have melted in the wind.

I want the hurt to disappear. I want to move forward. And so, I vow to be the one to start. "I'd like you both to come to Charleston soon. Come visit Ryder and me. We can get to know one another again." I look back to Ryder to make sure he's okay with my invite. He grins and winks. Pride and love shine brightly in his eyes for me. He's the hope and light I've been searching for, for so damn long. I couldn't have asked for a better man if I'd begged and pleaded with the Lord above.

Losing my son was the hardest thing I've ever been through in my life. Accepting Ryder's love even when I pushed him away so often was the smartest thing I've ever done. As much as I hate it, I'm not sure I'd have one without losing the other.

Lucas gave me hope.

Ryder gave me love.

Now, I have a peace I'd never dreamed of.

CHAPTER 23
Codie

I'm biting my lip so hard, I'm shocked I haven't split it. "Ryder," I groan into his hand as he licks at my pussy from behind. This man is insatiable.

"Quiet," he snaps at me. His frustration of the last four days is obvious.

We left my parents' after visiting for three days and came home to his parents still at his house, so we've been staying at mine. Only Nix's little sister, Lola, is in town, too, and needed a place to stay.

Wanting to be more involved with Ryder's work family, I offered up my spare room. She arrived two days ago and will be here for at least another three.

I really like her. Lola is funny, smart, and she enjoys

picking on her big brother. Which amuses me to no end after dealing with his shitty attitude for so long.

However, with all these people around, Ryder has held off on taking me the way we both desperately crave.

Hard, hot, and fast.

Tonight, he broke down when I gave him a look.

Or so he says. I don't know what this look was.

But as soon as Nix left and Lola went to bed, he locked our door and stripped me naked. Now, his face has been buried between my legs for at least an hour, and my body is exhausted. My brain is fried, and I don't think I could move if I tried.

Pushing his hand off my mouth, I plead, "Please, Ryder. I need you inside of me. I need to feel you rocking in and out. I need you."

"Dove, if I can get in this sweet little cunt, I'm never leaving. Not anytime soon, anyways." I can feel his lips as they move, and I barely hear a word he says.

"Ryder Morrison, if you don't fuck me good and proper right this minute, you won't see me naked for a month." That gives him pause as his tongue freezes from tickling my nub further.

"That's unfair," he growls, and I can feel the vibrations through my pussy, up into my womb, and then my breasts.

"What you're doing is unfair," I groan as I finally feel him pull away and sit up.

With one hand on my hip and the other gripping my hair, he slowly pushes his throbbing cock into my channel, and the fit is as tight as the first time because he's got me so worked up.

"Relax, woman." He grunts, slowly pushing in and out. After a few minutes, he's finally seated all the way inside me, and we both sigh with satisfaction. Pulling me up by the grip he has in my hair, he asks, "Do you know how much I love you?" His hoarse voice in my ear sends shivers racing down my spine as he gently pumps his hips up and down.

"Tell me," I plead.

The hand on my hip releases, and I have to hold onto his thighs to stay in this position as he murmurs, "More than life. More than the sun, the moon, and the stars." My heart beats rapidly in my chest. "My love for you is endless, Codie Ray." He turns my head so I'm looking back and up at him. "I love you with every fiber of my being, and there isn't a single person in the world I'd like to threaten me with no nudity for giving her too many orgasms than you." More damn tears. "Will you marry me?" I feel a cool band slip onto my finger, and when he holds our hands up, mine over his, I sob. Hard.

So hard I knock us off balance, and suddenly, I'm

flat on my stomach again, and he's deeper inside of me. Our hands still twined as he waits on my answer.

"I'm not moving until you say something," he murmurs as he kisses along my neck and cheek, licking up the tears as they cascade freely.

"Yes. Of course, yes!" My answer would never be anything else. This man is my absolute heart and soul.

Ryder

She said yes.

I watched Codie sleep all night after that. I couldn't take my eyes off of her. I wasn't certain she was even going to say yes, but I knew I couldn't not ask her. Not anymore. I may have never been impulsive before in my life, but with her, I want everything there is to experience, and I had to seal it with a ring on her finger.

With my parents here, plus Lola, I'd been starving for Codie. The need to hear her sweets sighs as I consumed her was a driving force I couldn't ignore after she sent me a look so filled with love that my heart constricted in my chest.

Emptying the carafe for coffee, I refill it and get to

work on making her breakfast. I've learned a thing or two about that woman this past week, and it's that if I don't make her breakfast, she rarely eats it.

Codie can get so absorbed in doing something that she completely forgets to nourish herself. It's a habit I aim to break.

"Good morning!" Lola prances in the room with her blonde hair a wild tangle on top of her head.

"Did a rat nest up there or something?" I point to her head and smirk as she lifts her hands to mess with it.

"Shut up, Ryder. Nix isn't here, you don't have to tease me." It's cute she thinks that's why I do it. We all love Lola; she's part of the family. Shitty for her that she has Nix plus us four big, overbearing pseudo-brothers who quite enjoy busting her chops.

"Don't need him here to do that." I laugh at her pout. She's a good kid. Keeps Nix insane and in his place when she visits, which is more entertaining than teasing her.

"Well, if somebody'd of kept it down last night, I wouldn't have slept with a pillow over my head." She cocks her head and hip in the same manner and eyes me up and down. "Did you break her?"

"Better." I grin.

"Oh yeah, how so?"

"I asked her to marry me."

"No way!" She squeals and jumps into my arms, strangling me with her hug. "She said yes, right? She'd be a fool not to. You know what, don't answer that. Obviously, she did or you two wouldn't have been up all night." Winking, she pulls away and grabs a coffee before I have a chance to.

"She did." The fucking look in her eyes when I asked her and slipped the ring on her finger, it's one I'll keep with me forever.

"Your mom is going to be thrilled!" Even though this was the first time Mom and Dad have met Lola, they hit it off instantly. Without parents of her own, I'm happy to share mine with the pain in the ass. "Hayes is going to flip out!"

"About what?" Codie walks into the kitchen in nothing but my t-shirt and a fuzzy pair of socks, looking sexy as hell.

"Jesus, woman." My dick is instantly hard for her. "Come here." Her smile is shy as Lola watches with awe in her eyes.

"You two are the sweetest thing ever," Lola sighs as I ignore her and lean down to kiss Codie.

Sucking her tongue into my mouth, I drag her body closer as she moans into my kiss, rubbing her hands under my shirt and up my chest. "Good morning," she whispers as I pull back slightly.

"Oh my god, you're killing me here!" Lola is two

years younger than Codie and has zero control of her emotions or mouth, so I'm not surprised about her impatience.

Codie, however, is. "What?" she asks.

"Your ring! I want to see it!" A blush creeps up Codie's neck as she pulls back and walks over to Lola. "It's gorgeous!"

"I love it, too." Codie's voice is quieter, but the excitement and love in it aren't missed by me.

"When's the big day?" Lola's impatience is going to get on my nerves.

"As soon as I can get her down the aisle." I smirk at Codie's shocked expression. For me, the sooner, the better. This woman is my entire life, and there's nothing more I'd love than to get her tied to me as soon as possible.

EPILOGUE

Ryder

Three months later.

Too long. It took too fucking long to get her down the aisle, but Codie wanted something special. Something for us to remember. It didn't matter that I told her I'd remember the day she took my name past death. And after Hayes and Levi had their little boy, Hayes begged us to wait a couple of months until she could be part of the wedding. It's no shocker that she and Codie have become the best of friends now.

But now, she's mine.

"Ryder, slow down." Her breathless voice is full of anticipation as we leave the reception hall, and I drag her up to our hotel room.

"Nope. Need you now." Hayes and Lola tortured me when they chose Codie's wedding dress. My wife had no idea what she wanted, but those girls tackled it like it was the fucking super bowl.

Silk. Nothing but silk upon silk. And it is all fucking see-through except for where she damn well better be covered. The front is high in the chest, and the sleeves are long, but there is no back to her dress. Everything's on display from the sweet curve of her sexy ass to the soft line of her neck.

The flare out from mid-thigh down is a vibrant lilac that trails behind her and makes her look like an angel. With her long brown hair twisted in a braid around her head, Codie looks more like a princess than anything else.

One I'm going to enjoy making scream my name all night long. "Here we are." I've barely got the key in the door before I'm ripping my white suit off and tossing the clothes across the room.

Codie stands before me, watching with an amused expression as I lose control. "I love when you're like this," she whispers as the sleeves on her dress slowly slide down her arms.

"Are you trying to kill me?" I groan, ready to pounce on her like a lion taking his mate. "You are, aren't you? Fucking Lola." That woman is a menace.

"I just want it to be special." She gazes up at me with

heat and love in her stare, and my heart rate finally slows down.

"Anything you want, dove." After the stress of the past few months and watching as her ex, Jason, dealt with his father's actions and subsequent incarceration, I'll give her whatever the fuck she wants.

"I just want you, Ryder." She smiles up at me and drops her dress. It slides down her body in a whoosh to reveal she has been completely naked underneath.

"Jesus." Every time I see her naked is like the first time, and I never know where to start. Pulling her into my arms, I lay light kisses along her collarbone and savor each breathy sigh, all her moans. I need to hold them close to me because tomorrow we leave on a new mission for the first time since rescuing her, and while I'm not worried about Codie anymore, I'm going to fucking miss her like crazy.

Codie

I never thought I'd be able to dream about being a wife again. I didn't think I would deserve the chance. But Ryder is always proving me wrong. In fact, he enjoys it.

Now, as he kisses every inch of flesh he can, I close my eyes and store each loving touch into my memory. I'm going to enjoy our wedding night together. Our last night with each other for a few days or weeks—he never knows for sure—until I can hold him in my arms again.

"Ryder," I sigh and arch into his body as his hands brush my thighs. His mouth captures a turgid nipple in his mouth, and the pleasure that explodes through my body is something I can never get enough of.

"Hold me, dove." His hands push my thighs apart as mine grip his hips. Fingers digging in as I anticipate his entrance to my core. I love the feel of him bare inside of me, and I would be lying if I didn't say that I do hope, one day, his seed will plant deeply in my womb. I would love nothing more than to give him a child. As much as it scares me, it also thrills me to create a life with Ryder.

"I love you," I gasp as his hips slowly rock back and forth as he forges forward and captures my body in moments of bliss only he can deliver to me.

"I'll never tire of hearing those words." He groans into my ear. His hands pull mine up to hold beside my head. My thighs grip him tight to my body as we make slow love.

"Promise you'll come back to me," I beg. I won't let my fear enter this realm but hearing his promise will help me cope while he's gone.

"I'll always come back to you, dove." He rests his forehead against mine, and our eyes lock in an unbreakable hold as we spread our love with our bodies.

"Always," I whisper into the quiet night, only broken up by our moans and our promises of forever with each other.

"I love you, Codie Morrison, with my entire being." Ryder's lips brush mine as we come together, and euphoria holds us long through the night in preparation for what the future holds.

The End

ACKNOWLEDGMENTS

Just a general shoutout to anyone who has asked for Ryder's story. Even though it's not all about him, I think you'll love it anyways!

ABOUT THE AUTHOR

Krystal is a proud Canadian girl, hailing from Sherwood Park, Alberta. She has a strong dislike for the winter, and a love for spring. Married to her husband Steve, for 15 years, they have 4 beautiful red headed spawns ranging in ages 7-13. She has a strong love of coffee, sarcasm, and wine. (Not necessarily in that order either.)

Krystal loves to write about instalove between couples looking for love. She has a passion for contemporary romance and springs into menage as often as she can.

For in the moment updates you can join her reader group – KL'S FIGHTERS.

Fractured Love (Early 2020)

Tarnished Love (Summer 2020)

The In His Arms Series

Safe, In His Arms

Coached, In His Arms (2019)

Bullied, In His Arms (2019)

Those Malcolm Boys

Obsessive Addiction

Accidental Obsession

Arrogantly Obsessed

Daniels Family

Until Arsen

With Kol

Before Noah (2020)

Love Letters

Dear Killian

Dear Gage

Dear Maverick

Dear Desmond

Dear Lena

Coming Soon

Until Hale (October 2019 in Aurora Rose Reynolds Until World)

Finished Series

The Adair Empire

King

Luther

Castiel

Atticus

Carver

Grasping For Air

Hogan Brother's

One Chance

One Choice

Unchained

The Possessed Series

OWNED by Dominic

One Dance for Case

Lost & Found

Lucky Christmas

The Protectors Series

Keeley's Fight

Emily's Protectors

Kennedy's Redemption

Stand Alone Titles

Mr. & Mrs.

Brantley's Way

Printed in Poland
by Amazon Fulfillment
Poland Sp. z o.o., Wrocław